Irrepressible

A Novel

Jacklyn Lee

Inspiring Publishers
P.O. Box 159, Calwell, ACT Australia 2905
Email: publishaspg@gmail.com
http://www.inspiringpublishers.com

A catalogue record for this
book is available from the
National Library of Australia

National Library of Australia The Prepublication Data Service

Author: Jacklyn Lee
Title: Irrepressible
Genre: Fiction, Comedy

Paperback ISBN: 978-1-923449-26-8

To my friends and family,
I hope this novel goes some way towards explaining things.
Or perhaps it will leave you even more
confused about things.
Either way, it'll do something.

PREFACE

This novel contains several characters who engage in crossdressing. These characters are based on my own experiences, and it should be noted that there are many different motivations behind crossdressing. This book can not possibly represent them all. I wrote most of this novel while I was still very much in a gender-questioning phase and still considered myself a crossdresser. I no longer think that and have since come out as non-binary and transgender. My point of view on gender has shifted since the first draft of this novel and although I no longer agree with them, I have retained a lot of those original perspectives. I think the mindset of a gender-confused person is worth sharing. Please don't pass judgments on or make presumptions about crossdressers or other gender-diverse people based on what I have written here.

The very term crossdressing might be considered inappropriate in some contexts. People might use the word crossdressing, where a phrase such as "dressing to reflect one's gender identity accurately" might be better. Alternatively, those who believe society's gender roles are a bit silly might just use the phrase: wearing clothes. But I use the term crossdressing as, while not perfect, it is the word the characters in the story would use.

Names, characters, businesses, places, events, locales and incidents are either the products of the author's imagination or used in a fictitious manner. Any resemblance to actual persons, living or dead, or actual events is purely coincidental. So, I guess just ignore that whole "based on my own experiences" part from before.

I would like to acknowledge the traditional owners of the land on which this novel was written, the lands of the Ngunnawal and Ngambri Nations. Portions of it were also written on the lands of the Wiradjuri Nation. I would also like to pay my respects to elders past and present. Sovereignty was never ceded.

CHAPTER 1

Men, four of them in particular, stood around the fire. "I don't know whose idea it was to go camping in June," said one of the men, soon to be identified as Stan. "It's fucking freezing out here."

"Oh harden up, Stan, it's not that cold," said Bart. It had been his idea to go camping in June. "And you think we'd have this place to ourselves in summer?"

The four of them were encamped in a slither of a national park that bordered the suburb they all called home, Pax Gardens.

"Ourselves?" exclaimed Joe. "I can see your house from here."

"Oh, barely."

"Rosalind is waving at me through the window."

"She is? Damn it! I told her not to disturb us on our weekend of manliness."

"Manliness? We're ten metres from camping in your backyard like a bunch of kids!"

"We're not in my backyard. We are deep in the wilderness surviving like men!" Bart insisted.

"Gentlemen, please," said Tim as he produced four beers from the esky which, considering how cold it was, was more decorative than anything else. "Can we stop bickering and get down to business?" Four beers were quickly accepted.

Tim raised his beer and calmly declared a toast: "To the Dregs."

"To the Dregs," the others said in unison.

They had been called the Dregs for as long as they could remember being friends. As children, they'd generally gotten up to no good. Many people, places and things had been broken, shattered, set on fire or lightly soiled due to their actions. As a result, adults started to refer to them as "the dregs of society". So, to spite said authority figures, they adopted the title officially. And with what spite they had left over, they all managed to do relatively well in their adult lives just to make sure that their adopted title would become ironic. But their appetite for breaking, igniting and soiling things hadn't diminished with age, and so every month or two, these Weekends of Manliness were organised. Previous weekends had included paintball, skydiving, the illegal manufacturing, acquisition and use of fireworks and that weekend where a poorly phrased Google search[1] for a barbeque festival ended up with them accidentally attending a gay spa.

The men tried the beer and looked slightly puzzled, "Well, that's, ah…" Stan paused before deciding on the word. "…an interesting choice. Tim, what is it?"

"It's a Dutch-Italian brown ale created with a genetically engineered strain of wheat, using hops that are first digested by some small rodents only found in a small part of the Amazon rainforest before being added to the brewing process," he explained, wondering for a moment if the craft beer trend was getting out of hand.

---

[1] Stan, to this day, maintains that "men's meat festival" sounded better.

"Yes, you can, uh, definitely taste the hops," said Stan.

"Yes, well, nice choice Tim. How long did it take you to pick it?" asked Joe.

"What do you mean?"

"You're pretty fussy when it comes to beer. I bet you were there deciding the whole night."

"Well, not the whole night," said Tim as he looked over to another part of the bushland.

⌇

A few nights earlier Tim had been pacing back and forth in his living room. He was done, he decided. Definitely. Absolutely. For good this time. Not like the other fifteen times he had definitely been done. This time he was absolutely done, so that made it different. Absolutely is a much more definitive word than definitely, so it was sure to work this time. He stopped pacing and looked at his watch. It was a few hours before Julia finished her shift. It shouldn't take that long, but Tim had done this enough times to know that nurses' shifts could be cut short if the patient load was light. He would pick up some beer on the way back. That way, if Julia got home before him, he could cover by saying he'd been out preparing for the weekend of manliness. The bottle shop wouldn't be open much longer, so he had to move.

Going into the bedroom, he found everything where he'd left it. His new favourite dresses were draped over the bedsheets. Several different bras and cup-filling socks were strewn across the floor. The ensuite was a mess. The sink, full of used makeup wipes, was bordered by open containers of powder, lipsticks, several mascara wands and a pile of brushes. An entire woman had been painstakingly constructed here several hours ago and then thoroughly deconstructed a few hours later. It smelled of a mix of burnt hair from one too many attempts to use a hair straightener to get her hair just right and nail polish remover from far too much time spent scrubbing his nails back to their boring normal colour. Next to the bed, a pile of high heels littered the floor. They had been bought anonymously online in bulk in the hope that one pair might be anywhere close to fitting.

He pulled a large, newly purchased duffle bag out of the closet, slapped on a pair of latex gloves and got to work. Tim was a police officer and, while in training, had worked part time for a forensic crime scene cleanup crew for extra credit. He knew exactly what traces from the crime scene lying in front of him could lead people back to him. First, any traces of makeup would be thoroughly dissolved with a mixture of solvents. Then, the whole house would be completely vacuumed to make sure any fibres, loose tags, buttons or other traces of shame that could be discovered by a fashion-aware adversary were removed. As a bonus, it made him look like an excellent boyfriend as the house would be spotless.

As he started scrubbing away at the bathroom, he wondered if it was really worth the effort to keep the crossdressing a secret. Julia would probably understand. She was fairly progressive. When they'd first met in university, she'd been quite radical. Riots on campus were known as Julias. She didn't so much upset the apple cart as flip it over and set it on fire. The university had almost expelled her when during one animal rights

protest, she had attempted to neuter a molecular biology professor responsible for live animal testing. She claimed it would make him more empathetic towards his subjects. If anything, Tim was worried about Julia finding out about the crossdressing because she might go on some gender equality crusade and make him embrace it. Sometimes, she could take things too far. He didn't want to take this thing to a neutering level.

Equally, he wasn't concerned about his work. There were new diversity awareness programs and training these days, so it was doubtful he would be fired. Even then, he could find a new job if he had to, but he doubted any organisation like the police would risk an unfair dismissal case over this.

But the Dregs? That bastion of manliness? The group that almost adopted "men doing manly men things" as its official motto?[2] He couldn't imagine this being accepted there. Maybe he could live without his girlfriend or his job but not without them. He couldn't even remember life without The Dregs. Their bond was as strong as blood, literally, after one weekend of manliness where they had all gotten blood transfusions together to become blood brothers and cement their bond.[3] He couldn't lose them he thought as he stuffed another dress into his duffle bag.

Disposal was an issue. Everyone knew that Skevy Sully, who ran the local tip, went through everything. He couldn't simply throw out the duffle bag when he was done. Tim had spent a lot of time in training going over murder case studies and had been involved on the periphery of a few cases, and he took inspiration from them. In his opinion, what he was disposing of was far more shameful than a dead body. Tim could think of several instances where the police knew the body was probably buried in bushland somewhere but it was never located, and Pax Gardens was conveniently located

---

[2] It lost out to "Better Off Dreg". Other runners up included "Make Australia Dreg Again", "Dreg and Loving It" and "Once You Go Dreg You Never Go Back".

[3] Surprisingly, only two had gotten blood poisoning.

next to a national park. He threw the bag and a shovel in the back seat of his car, set his GPS for a nicely isolated spot and set off into the night. As he pulled up to his destination, the only sign of any recent activity was tyre tracks from the last time he'd been here. There was no one around for miles except for himself and the stars, and he wished they would get lost. He didn't want any witnesses, no matter how many lightyears away.

Tim used to mock murderers at work. Why were bodies always found in shallow graves? He joked that if he were a murderer, he would bury his victims in deep graves. Now that he had actually tried digging graves for the remains of his weekend adventures as Brooke, he understood. Digging graves was really hard. Shallow graves were good enough. It didn't take long to dig the hole, and he hurled in the bag. As he shovelled the dirt back on, Tim tried to guess how many bags of his clothes must be buried around there. He'd lost count. It was probably time to find a new dumping ground. No wait, this was the last time. He wouldn't need to do this again. Dusting himself off, he got back to the car. Plenty of time before the bottle shop closed.

The liquor store was almost empty. The owner sat behind the register and watched as Tim spent far too long deciding exactly what kind of beer he wanted. He painstakingly took out bottles to hold up to the light to judge the colour before putting them back and moving to another part of the fridge. Alcohol. It was hard to think of a liquid that had changed the course of history more. Some would argue for oil,[4] but it had been around a mere century or two. Alcohol was ancient. Roman armies were fuelled by amphoras of wine, Egyptian

---

[4] Some smart alecs would also say water.

slaves by a primitive form of beer. Even the meetings of the allied leaders in the Second World War were said to be reasonably boozy affairs. It had certainly changed the course of Tim's life. It was there when he first kissed a girl. It was there when he first did more than kiss a girl. It was there when he graduated. It was there when he gave the best man's speech at Bart's wedding.[5] It was there to soften the grief when his childhood dog died. Other than the Dregs, it had probably been at his side longer than anything else. And it had been useful.

Fitting in was always hard when you had secretive hobbies like Tim's. Alcohol offered a shared experience, and Tim embraced it. Starting in high school and continuing through university, Tim had steadily built a reputation as the craziest of the crazies. At every party, Tim was there, and the following day everyone would be talking about the latest ridiculous story involving Tim. If a bodily fluid had been deposited somewhere inappropriate, Tim was involved. If something or someone had been set on fire, Tim was implicated. If a national monument and/or cemetery was desecrated, Tim had a hand in it.[6] If someone mentioned Tim, the first thing they would think of was one of his alcohol-fuelled exploits. Someone who likes to dress up like a woman in his spare time would not be anybody's first thought. All of this was a good cover, but it was also a lot of fun. And it was how he met Julia. Her radical side led to a relatively liberal attitude to drugs. Their first dates were mostly raves, or so they suspected. Neither one remembered that time period well.

---

[5] As you can imagine, the title "Best Man" was hotly contested amongst The Dregs, and Tim did a lot of backstabbing to get it.

[6] The author would like to remind people that this book is a work of fiction, and any resemblance of these events to reality is purely coincidental. Also, you can't prove anything.

There was simply a time they remembered being single, a blank spot of several months, and then they were in a serious long-term relationship.

Tim had picked out an interesting case of craft beer for the Dregs, but now he needed to get something for himself. He would need it if tonight really were going to be the last time. After a pint or two, he always felt better. There was no obsessive searching through online shoe stores trawling for something that looked gorgeous and would actually fit him. No comparing his calendar to Julia's shift roster to figure out the next time he could dress up and go out. Tim wasn't sure exactly how it worked, but somehow, alcohol inhibited whatever part of his brain made him want to crossdress, and he could just feel, well, normal. He could just hang out on the couch with Julia and watch a miniseries or read a book and not worry about shame or gender identity or anything like that.

Some people might claim he was an alcoholic, and Tim wouldn't necessarily dispute that. But he didn't consider it the worst of his vices. Going cold turkey on crossdressing was hard enough. God knows what would happen if he cut out beer at the same time. And anyway, alcoholism was a much more socially acceptable addiction. As Joe would say, the trick was to market it properly. No one wants to hang out with a drunk, but everybody loves a party animal.

The bottle shop owner finally decided to walk over. "Need any help?"

Tim thought about the question for a good few seconds, staying focused on the fridge, "No, I'm just trying to figure out what I want."

◦‿◦

Stan looked in the mirror and sighed. This made no damn sense at all. Stan was a scientist. His field of expertise was so specialised that it would take half an hour to give you the gist of it, so we won't bother. The point is that he is a very logical and reasonable man. So, things that made no sense irked him. They got under his skin and gnawed away at his insides until they made sense or he forced them to. The fact that the red velvet "Ravishing Rouge" lipstick from an obscure cosmetics outlet in Italy, applied with the precision of a 3D printer to both lips, perfectly matching the equally precise application of reddish-brown "Hazy Hazelnut" eyeshadow he also had on, and the fact that all of this made deliriously happy, irked him. Why should the basic, if not expertly applied, chemicals plastered to his face make him feel anything at all except slightly cold and moist at the application points? Not to mention the ridiculous colour scheming. Matching things was very difficult when the colours had ridiculous names such as "Pouty Plum", "Smitten Kitten" and "Flirty Fuchsia". Couldn't they use the standard computer hexadecimal encoding scheme for colours? He'd resorted to buying several different colours of each piece of makeup for his planned design and then testing all of them with a colourimeter he'd bought to get the exact colour he wanted. Online makeup tutorials talked about matching skin tones with vague terms such as "warm tones" and "cool tones". They delineated regions of the face as triangles without specifically defining any lengths or angles. There was plenty more such pseudoscientific nonsense. There was no precision at all, just people choosing things based on feelings! It was entirely illogical, but nonetheless, he devoured all these tutorials and practised incessantly.

He wondered if maybe, as a logical man, that the illogical was the last taboo for him. Perhaps the erotic appeal of the novelty could be what compelled his unreasonable behaviour. Stan looked down on psychology as a lesser science, if it was a science at all. Yet neuroscience was still in its infancy, meaning that he would never have a hope of knowing what motivated him. He sighed, causing a curl of chestnut brown hair to fall over his face. He inspected it intensely before brushing it aside. Stan's long hair was usually ill-maintained and tied up in a greasy geeky ponytail. But when he got dressed up, it was his hair that made most biological women jealous. Days were spent expunging the grease and conditioning it with a vast array of hair products before he curled it expertly into perfect waves which he had calculated precisely using complex differential geometry. It was a lot of effort, but the result made him tremendously and nonsensically happy.

What made less sense than the joy was the shame, especially because he often felt them simultaneously, which he felt made the use of emotions to communicate information from the subconscious to the conscious mind pretty useless. If he ever found the designers of his brain, he would have a long conversation with them about the standardisation of protocols.

But he also knew, at least on the surface, there was no real shame in what he was doing. He should be able to put any non-reactive chemical substance on his face that he wanted to. Well, okay, he thought, he could probably explain away the makeup. The red dress and heels, on the other hand, were trickier. They had been painstakingly selected from several online stores to fit his body shape and match the lipstick to within a few nanometres of the wavelength of their colour, which probably also contributed to the shame. But the argument remained: Why are these the domain of women? The answer, of course, was that there was no reason. Stan knew it was solely because of illogical societal constructs[7] that this was forbidden, and there was nothing wrong with wearing women's clothing. The shame made no sense. But what made even less sense was that if it were deemed that how he was dressed right now was acceptable to society, he probably wouldn't enjoy it as much. The erotic appeal of the novelty would be gone. He was stuck in a Catch-22 of crossdressing, gender norms and sexuality. It had to be solved. He had to stop now, or he would be exposed. That's what the interview had shown him.

∽

"Can you confirm this is a copy of your birth certificate?" A voice boomed at Stan from behind the lamp.

"Well, not really. You're kind of shining a bright light in my face," Stan replied.

The interrogator looked flummoxed by Stan's response. Stan could tell that the light was an important part of the man interrogation strategy and he was not used to being called out on it. The interrogator managed to unflummox his face and silently slid the certificate over the flimsy metal table between them in an imposing manner.

They were sitting in a small room, the desk and chairs being the only furnishings. Stan was impressed by the blandness of it all. Nothing but off-white shades and a general aura of blandness that seemed beyond reason. Stan, a minimalist, could only dream of his apartment reaching this level of bland.

He eyeballed the document. It was indeed his birth certificate. A quick check of where the sex was recorded showed it still said male. It was good to check it every now

---

[7] Well, okay, maybe they were logical if you were trying to subdue the female element of your population into servitude and, of course, you were a man.

and then, Stan thought, just in case someone had read it wrong the first time. It might explain some things. "Yes, that's mine."

"Can you confirm you were born in Pax Gardens General Hospital on the thirty-first of March, nineteen eighty-nine?"

"That's what it says here."

"But can you confirm it?"

"Well, the certificate does that."

"Yes, but I'm asking you to confirm it."

Stan looked around the room as if there might be something to tell him how to respond to this, "Well, I don't really remember it."

"You can't confirm it?"

"It was a bit of a stressful day. Met lots of new people, including one I had just been extracted from." This response was met with a steely cold silence. "I could get some witnesses if you want?"

"That won't be necessary." The interrogator appeared to be happy enough that he had re-established his authority after his earlier flummox and that the subject was once again suitably intimidated. "Mr Enmore, as you have applied to work for a sensitive area of DätaCorp[8] you need a high-level security clearance. This is simply the first of several security assessments, no need to worry."

"Several?" Stan was beginning to regret the aforementioned application to DätaCorp. But his field of expertise was highly specialised and obscure and this meant not a huge number of people would pay a living wage for his skills. His choices were either supervillainy or working for an IT giant. DätaCorp and the other IT giants were arguably only one step away from

---

[8] It was pronounced the same as data. The umlaut had been added as a measure to avoid copyright issues while the company crushed the hundreds of other companies also called DataCorp.

supervillainy. Still, they seemed to have some sort of legal backing, so it was a safer choice and slightly more socially acceptable than full-blown supervillainy. Given other parts of his life, he didn't need anything more socially unacceptable. He couldn't back out now anyway. DätaCorp were clients of Joe's firm, and he had gone out of his way to get him an interview. Joe would be pretty upset with him if he wasted his client's time.

"Yes, we have to be thorough," continued the investigator. "There are all sorts of investigations we need to conduct. Financial, psychological, medical, geological, astrological."

"Astrological?"

"Yes, I mean, we wouldn't want to hire a Libra when Neptune is rising into Capricorn, would we?"

Stan looked at the man for a few seconds, but his expression remained serious. "Right… Well, at least that has more sense behind it than a polygraph,"[9] Stan joked.

"Oh, we do those too."

"Oh... good."

"Worried, are you?"

"No, not really." This was the truth. Stan knew that if they discovered his proclivities for ultrafeminine expeditions, they might reconsider hiring him. These tests were designed to make sure the employees of DätaCorp were people of the utmost integrity and moral fortitude. In reality, they made sure that DätaCorp hired only the very best liars. And Stan was an excellent liar. His tactic was simple: he was generally honest and tried to tell the truth. This meant if he ever needed to lie, people would believe him.

---

[9] The polygraph has been debunked as a lie detector several times. Despite this, it remains in use for vetting employees in several organisations who apparently think that the only thing more unreliable than a polygraph is trusting people.

Stan was also meticulous when it came to covering the tracks of his time as Loreta. He had amassed a small, untraceable fortune through speculative bitcoin trading. The fortune was used to finance a series of PO boxes spread around town, each set to forward mail to another in a giant loop. When ordering feminine supplies online, he would simply wait for the package to be shipped between two PO boxes with poor security and then assist the package in falling off the back of a truck. Since the package was for him anyway, no one ever reported it stolen, least of all the post office staff responsible for it. They didn't want to deal with that paperwork. His outings as Loreta were at locations not known to anyone connected to him and with minimal security cameras. After an adventure as Loreta, he would scrub his entire house with a cocktail of disinfectants and dump everything in a brick-loaded bag at the bottom of the river before scrubbing himself with said disinfectants. He was confident that DätaCorp wouldn't find anything on him, except maybe a few chemical burns from the disinfectants.[10]

"And of course," continued the interrogator, "there's the phallometry test."

"I'm sorry, the what test?" Stan liked to think of himself as an educated man who knew most Latin sounding scientific words, but this one eluded him.

"Phallometry. It's kind of like a polygraph, but it measures the blood flow to the genitals."

Stan looked confused in the general direction of the man, "Why on earth would you want to do that?"

"Because when a human being such as yourself gets aroused, there is an increase in blood flow to the penis. So if

---

[10] Luckily, several Weekends of Manliness had also resulted in chemical burns, so he had a cover story for them.

you measure that blood flow while asking about a variety of sexual perversions, you can tell which perversions someone has."

Again, Stan scrutinised the interrogator, but he seemed serious. "Seems a little extreme, doesn't it? I mean, who cares what people do in their bedrooms, right?"

"Oh, we care. Imagine if one of our competitors or a foreign government discovered that you were into ummm…" The interrogator lacked much of an imagination when it came to these things. "Vegetables or something," he continued. "Would you honestly keep secrets from them when they're threatening to expose you?"

It was a terrible explanation, but Stan had to admit he had a point. He also had to admit this was a problem. The moment they asked how he felt wearing a dress, enough blood would flow down there that he would probably faint. "These phallometers, they can't be very accurate, can they? I mean, you couldn't cancel a clearance over one of these things, right?"

"Oh, the one we got is pretty good. This isn't one of those all volumetric mercury pressure tube ones," Stan tried for a moment to imagine how that could possibly work but decided it was probably best not to. "No, our one uses lasers to detect rapid changes in penile volume and measures the doppler shift in the blood. They're super-sensitive lasers, same ones they use to detect gravity waves. They're sensitive enough that they can pick up the arousal of a man looking at an avocado from over fifty metres away!"

"The machine can be that far away from the man?"

"No, the machine has to be strapped to the man. The avocado is fifty metres away."

"Ah, okay."

There was a brief silence before the interrogator added, "That's very impressive when you understand that arousal follows the inverse square law."

"Okay, but why an avocado?"

"Studies have shown it's the least sexy fruit or vegetable."

"Really? Avocado?"

"Yes, they're disgusting!" said the interrogator as he broke his usual calm demeanour, "I mean, look at them, inside or outside. Gross. Not like an onion. Now that we could pick up from orbit."

"An onion?"

"Yes, they're very sexy. I mean, they're so smooth yet so soft. You peel back layer, after layer, after... layer..." The interrogator had a pleasant smile on his face as he stared into the distance.

Stan looked around, wondering if this was a test before coughing loudly.

The interrogator snapped back to reality. "The point is that the system works. So, if you want to work for us, you'll have to do it."

"Sure. I have nothing to hide," lied Stan.

"That's the spirit. Now back to the matter at hand," the integrator brought up his list of questions to cover, "Have you ever had a relationship with a Scorpio in June?"

Stan's phallometry test was to take place in a few weeks. He looked down at the perfectly lacquered cherry red "Sexy Scarlet" nails on his hand and curled them into a fist. This had to be the last time. He had always felt a little on the outside of the other Dregs. They enjoyed their sports, mountain climbing, sex. By Joe's accounts, sometimes all three at once. Stan enjoyed maybe one of those.[11] His attempts to introduce more intellectual pursuits had never gone well. The poetry night he organised only led to a series of poems about how lame poetry nights were and several dirty limericks. The Dungeons and Dragons night had gone nowhere. Joe's character wouldn't leave the starting tavern until he had overly descriptive sex with everyone in the tavern while in the meantime, Tim's character had died from alcohol poisoning. The chess night had ended with Bart literally flipping the table, complaining that "I would have won if horses moved straight like they do in the fucking real world!"

But the Dregs had accepted him where others would decry him as a nerd. Being uncovered as a crossdresser when he was already the least Dreg-like would be a disaster. He couldn't lose them. There was only one option: he would have to cure himself. Luckily, there was something on his side: fear. It was a powerful force if used properly. Some more progressive opinions would say that he should be proud of his crossdressing identity, fly some sort of rainbow flag. Those people were wrong. Fear was there for a reason. It had kept humans alive for millennia. When you saw a tiger, you ran. You didn't stand there and show your pride. Sure, fighting off large mammalian predators was slightly different to wearing miniskirts in public, but Stan was confident. Nothing scared him more than losing the Dregs. He grabbed his Louis Vuitton purse and clacked his way out of the house.

⌒

She oozed femininity, Joe decided. Oozed was the word he had been trying to pin down. Oozed like puss leaking from

---

[11] Who doesn't like mountain climbing?

a boil: once you saw it you couldn't avoid looking at it. He had long ago lost track of the rankings of his conquests[12] but he estimated she would easily be in the top ten. Hell, probably even top five. Joe briefly left this train of thought to tell a hilarious joke[13] that had her laughing for more than a few seconds. A lesser woman would have done something uncouth at such hilarity like spit out some wine, have an annoying laugh, or let little bits of bacteria encrusted spittle fly from their gaping mouth, but not this woman. She laughed at just the right pitch, her laugh as pleasant as music, while she whipped her hair around stylishly. She was good, thought Joe, but he was better. This was what he did, and he did it well. Actually, not well. Well is how you would ask someone to cook your steak if you had no taste. Joe was a master. He worked in marketing, and the easiest product in the world to market was himself.

As far as Joe was concerned, he had fantastic features and an orgasm guarantee.[14] He pretty much sold himself. In the metaphorical sense, that is, not the sense that implies prostitution. The product he was selling did have one minor fault, at least in Joe's opinion. It had developed an inexpungible desire to dress up as a woman. Joe was never quite sure if this fault had occurred in the manufacturing process or because of some mishandling of the product after it had shipped, but it was there. Luckily it wasn't a visible defect, so Joe did what any good salesman would do: he didn't bring it up. It wasn't his fault if the customer didn't explicitly ask if the product occasionally puts on a dress and goes out on the town.

---

[12] Not because it was an especially large number. Joe was just bad at maths.

[13] The joke was so good that we won't sully its reputation by including it in this book amongst a bunch of second-rate jokes.

[14] Guarantee void in South Australia.

And besides, thanks to these dates, Joe mostly had the fault under control. It was akin to being an amateur athlete watching a professional. Of course, the amateur wishes it was them out on the field, being cheered on by the crowd and showered in champagne on the winner's podium. But the amateur knows what it would take to get to that level and is unwilling to give up what they would have to from all the other parts of their life. So, watching a professional at the top of their game was the closest you could get. You could admire their style and technique and perhaps think of how, one day, you could get anywhere close to their standard.

Right now, Joe was admiring a professional, specifically the gorgeous high heels she had on. They were a brand he had never heard of, but he was taken immediately. Whenever she got up to use the bathroom, Joe would close his eyes and imagine the clicking of her shoes on the tiles emanating from his own feet. Joe lived vicariously through his dates. This allowed him to control his urges. Some people might think he was using them, but Joe figured they got something out of it too. Women wanted him, and he wanted to be them.

The current woman was looking over the dessert menu. "You know," she said with a smirk, "I thought maybe we could skip dessert." She bit her lower lip seductively to drive home the point.

This made Joe flinch because he worried that she would ruin her flawless application of lipstick. Then he realised the implication was sex and stopped caring so much. "Sounds good to me. Let's get the bill."

"Yes, let's," she said and gave another seductive look designed to send him crazy. It did, but only because the look in question produced a lot of eyebrow movements. They looked terrific, and Joe fought off the desire to ask her where she'd got them done and if they took appointments for men.

For Joe, sex was simply a beneficial side effect of the whole process. He doubted he would pursue it as vigorously as he did if it weren't a way of dealing with what he considered his defect. Not only was it somewhat pleasurable, but it also provided a good cover story. The Dregs could never know that these dates were the methadone for his crossdressing. He severely doubted that a group of men who had, on one weekend of manliness, all taken plaster casts of their penises and competed to see who could sell the most dildos online[15] would be understanding when it came to this. Joe was not one to risk exile. He had previously gone to great lengths to prevent it.

One weekend of manliness, the Dregs had gone on a beach trip. It was only once they were at the beach that Joe had the horrifying realisation he had shaved his legs the week before on an outing as Josephine. The moment he went in the water, it would be obvious that his usually bear-like legs were now bare. His solution to this predicament was simple: he swam in his jeans. But, of course, this approach raised questions.

"Joe, are you wearing jeans in the ocean?" asked Stan.

"Oh, what these?" replied Joe, not sounding worried for an instant, "These are the new swim jeans a client of mine is developing. These are just a prototype, of course."

Stan thought for a moment. "That can't be a real thing."

"Yes, it is. I've been helping with the development."

"No you haven't."

"You'll see. They'll be on the shelves in a matter of months."

"Yeah, sure they will."

---

[15] Joe had finished in a respectable second place, which he considered pretty good considering the monstrosity that Bart had between his legs.

Joe was quick to pitch the idea to one of the clothing companies he did some consulting work for, and they were won over by the idea of expanding swimwear to the largely untapped body-conscious market. He made sure they rammed it through production so that they would be on the market when he told Stan. Several test subjects got mild brain damage when an early prototype caused them to sink like a stone. This would have destroyed a lesser man, but Joe quickly pronounced them a new product line: dive jeans. The swim jeans turned out to be a huge hit. Joe got a promotion. Stan admitted he was wrong. The test subjects settled for a large cash payout. And no one would ever suggest that Joe had shaved his legs in order to go crossdressing on weekends. Once again, he had used his marketing prowess to win the day.

And that's what the sex was: marketing. Joe made sure he engaged in all sorts of depraved acts with his dates[16] in order to have a stockpile of stories with which he could entertain the Dregs. Plenty of stories to confirm his status as one of the manliest of men. He didn't always want to take the sex to some of the stranger places it went, but he felt he had to, and sometimes the dates insisted. One particularly disturbing act, which Joe later found out was illegal in several states, made him so disgusted with himself he had actually thrown up during sex. But, of course, this just made a better story for the Dregs.

People didn't understand marketing, thought Joe. They thought it was just coming up with a slogan and slapping it on a billboard. But it took dedication and constant study. Joe was a master of the art of marketing, and he was his own

---

[16] Consensually, of course.

masterpiece. Well, that and the swim jeans. He won an award for that.

The sex was average.[17] Lying in bed with her afterwards, Joe tried to think of some colour he could add to it to keep it interesting when recounting the events to the Dregs. It was hard to concentrate when he had a direct line of sight to the women's clothing strewn across the floor. There was a spectacular front-hooking pink lace bra on the ground whose label he frustratingly couldn't see. He cursed his passionate way of ripping clothes off his dates. Screw it, he thought, I'll just tell them she wanted to do butt stuff. That usually makes them happy.

"I'm just going to freshen up," said his date before walking to the bathroom completely naked, taking an extra-long path across the room to show off her perfect body. Unfortunately, he wasn't paying attention as he struggled to make out the brand on the bottom of the heels that had been thrown to the other side of the room. She was in the bathroom a while. Joe never understood why women took so long to get ready. Sure, it took him several hours in there when he was trying to look like a woman, but he was starting from a very manly initial position. They already were women. What more did they need? Finally, the door to the ensuite cracked open, "I was thinking maybe we could get some brunch?" said a voice from within. Joe could only respond with a confused look, "Don't worry," she said, "I know what this is. I just feel like we could get a good breakfast out of it. I'll buy."

---

[17] In Chuck Palaniuk's book on writing *Consider This*, he says you should always describe the sex scenes. Chuck Palaniuk also spends his time writing stories about people losing organs during strange sex acts, which he then reads at book signing events and counts how many people faint. I feel his advice is optional.

Joe was surprised. Usually, his dates ended with him ignoring their calls for a while and maybe changing his phone number. He admired her pragmatism, and he had to admit he could use a good brunch.

She took him to a cafe not far from his apartment. It was a strange experience for Joe, being out with a woman in the daytime. In this light he could better appreciate the intricate details of her outfit, but as they sat down at their booth, he felt that something was off about the whole situation. Shortly a waiter appeared to take their order.

"I'll get an avo toast, thanks," said Joe.

His date let out a derisive laugh.

"What?"

"Avocado? Really?" said his date, "You know that's very last decade. Everyone's gone off them. You may as well be asking for mushy peas. I'll have a smashed onion on toast, thanks."

"That sounds worse."

"Are you kidding? The onions are in honey."

"Really?" He looked at the waiter, who nodded. Joe didn't want to risk his reputation with an unfashionable food choice, "Okay, I'll have what she's having."

His date busied herself on her phone while they waited for the food to arrive, which didn't take long. Joe experimentally poked his food with his fork. Before he could decide what to do with it, his date interrupted. "So tell me, Joe: how long exactly have you been a crossdresser?"

Joe looked at her in stunned silence.

"I found your stash in the crawl space above your ensuite. Took me a while to track it down while you slept. The mouse traps were a clever defence but they just served to tell me I was on the right track."

"I don't know what you're talking about," Joe finally stammered.

She threw a lipstick across the table, one of his favourite shades, "Need more proof?"

"That's not… I mean, I've never… I wouldn't," he continued to stammer.

"Oh Joe, such poor form compared to last night. I quite enjoyed the show. The jokes, the style, the suit. It was how I knew you were a good target. Anyone that well put together is hiding something. Gotta admit, though, never suspected crossdressing. You're good."

"Target?"

"Oh, figure it out, Joe. I'm a professional blackmailer. This is what I do. You think I could afford these clothes on the salary of the fake waitress job I told you I had?"

"Yes? I don't know. I didn't really think about it."

She sighed, "Of course you didn't. Let's just get to business, shall we? I'm going to need you to pay me fifty thousand dollars, or I'm going to tell everyone your secret. I gathered plenty of evidence while you were sleeping as well as all the contacts from your phone."

"Fifty thousand? I don't have that kind of money."

"Yes, you do. I did a valuation of your property and assets last night."

Joe slumped back in his chair. He didn't know what to do.

"Tell you what, Joe. I'll let you keep your money if you can do one thing for me."

"Sure anything, what?"

"Tell me: what's my name?"

Joe looked wide-eyed for a second and then in deep thought. "Kate?"

"It's Claire. Not bad for a complete guess, though." She laughed loudly. "I do that every time, and so far, not one of you has gotten it right."

Joe clenched his fist under the table. He wasn't going to go down like this. "Go ahead, tell everyone, I don't care. I've no wife or girlfriend to worry about, and I've been successfully estranging my family for years. You won't do any damage."

"Oh, I think I might," she said, suddenly taking on a much more serious tone, "You may not have any direct family but those friends of yours, the so-called Dregs – the way your eyes lit up when you talked about them, the way you wouldn't shut up about your stupid adventures with them – you obviously care about them. I think it may have been the only genuine thing about you last night. How do you think your macho little guy group will take this? Think they'll let you stick around once they find out you like to put on a dress, go out and get drilled by guys?"

"What?! I'm not gay."

She shrugged, "I was just testing. If you had been, I could have added another ten grand to the price."

"You're not just going to lie and say I'm gay?"

"No, in our industry, you've got to have a code of ethics."

"*Our* industry? I'm no blackmailer."

"Oh, but you are, Joe." She leaned forward, "You blackmail women all day with the products you market. You keep women trapped in the world of femininity. You tell them they have to use your products or people might discover their skin has a wrinkle or their complexion isn't perfect. They need name brand handbags so people won't think they're unfashionable. You're so good at this, you've even convinced yourself you need to be this idealised version of womanhood. You and I are the same. The difference is I'm honest about who I am. Well, at least with myself."

Joe searched for a witty reply but then decided just to say, "Go fuck yourself."

She laughed. "Oh, I will, with the diamond-encrusted dildo I buy with your money."

Joe winced a little. "That sounds painful."

"Yeah, true. Maybe a gold plated one… No! A platinum dildo. Yes, that's the right combination of expensive and non-jagged." An elderly couple at the next table gave them a strange look. She cleared her throat, "You have two weeks to gather the funds. I'll be in touch with the payment details. If you don't pay, an automated email will be sent to all the contacts I collected from your phone. My meeting with an unfortunate accident won't stop this, so don't get any ideas. Thanks for brunch, but I've got to get across town and threaten someone who is refusing to pay up," she said and started getting up.

"Wait, I thought you were paying?"

"Really?"

Joe simply sat and looked at her expectantly.

"Oh fine," she groaned and rolled her eyes. "I'll deduct it from your bill. You now owe me forty-nine thousand nine hundred and forty-two dollars and fifteen cents." She left Joe to think things over but only made it a few steps before turning back. "Oh Joe, by the way, don't try anything stupid like going to the police. I think this conversation should have conveyed that I'm much, much smarter than you and obviously have contingencies in place for such rash actions. Bye!"

Joe was left by himself at the table with nothing to do but tend to his bruised ego. He couldn't let her get away with this. She may have warned him against doing anything stupid, but she forgot something: he was a Dreg. Doing stupid things was what they did. As a result of many Weekends of Manliness, he had been burned, beaten, battered, poisoned, catheterised, arrested, baptised and shaved more often than he would like to remember. And he'd always survived. Joe got up and left the cafe to think of what act of stupidity would be best fitted for this situation. He kind of liked the burned, beaten and battered options but the situation called for something more subtle.

∾

You, Bart told himself, are a man. This is just a necessity. His heels clicked on the tiles as he wafted through the mall, leaving a trail of Chanel No. 5. He felt his dress straining under his armpits, clearly not designed for his overly broad shoulders, while also wondering if it was too short for him as he self-consciously pulled it downwards. You're a man, he told himself again. You sometimes get these urges and they have to be dealt with. Bart allowed himself to indulge in a little crossdressing every now and then because he counterweighted it with excessive masculinity. When averaged out over enough time, this plunge into femininity barely affected his man credentials. Bart did everything he could to confirm his status. He played five different weekend sports. In one rugby competition, he was so keen he signed up for two teams. It was awkward when they played each other, but Bart made it fair by randomly tackling anyone he felt like during the match. He ran mara, bi, tri and quadrathlons. He brewed beer and drank fine scotch, often with a cigar in hand. He was a regular gym junkie. Not that Bart knew what people were supposed to do at the gym. He turned up, hung around, picked up a heavy-looking object or two, spent two minutes on a treadmill and left. But when people at work asked him what he got up to yesterday, he could proudly say he went to the gym. He grew beards of various designs. When a crossdressing urge came on and he was forced to shave, he simply told people he was sick of hiding his finely chiselled jawline.

Bart had once read that the ratio of your left-hand index finger to your right-hand middle finger was directly correlated to how much testosterone you had been exposed to in the womb. Thus many hours were spent filing down his middle finger. For years he slept with a small rack on this index finger, slowly attempting to extend it. Stan told him this was junk science that had been disproven years ago. The ratio was essentially meaningless. This didn't stop Bart. Society had decided that the finger ratio was a measure of one's manhood, just as it had done with penis length, muscle volume and chest hair density.[18] Without such measures, how could anyone be sure of their man status? It was like that cat in a box stuff Stan was always talking about, thought Bart. Until you opened the box, the cat was both alive and dead. Bart viewed gender the same way. There had to be some way to measure it. Otherwise, how could anyone be sure of who they were?

While he maintained this impressive resume of manliness, he also made sure to defend it vigorously. One time while out shopping with Rosalind, she forced him to buy some sort of strawberry smelling shampoo designed for "luscious hair" when the usual brand that Bart bought, the one that had "for men" prominently displayed on the bottle, was out of stock. The resulting fracture from the impromptu extreme paragliding session that afternoon took five weeks to heal. Sometimes the best defence was a good offence. When Bart had been trimming his fingernails for an upcoming mountain

---

[18] The experimental nighttime rack for increasing penis length was an experience Bart did not want to revisit anytime soon.

climbing expedition, Joe made a joke, asking if Bart wanted to paint them afterwards. The resulting fracture from the impromptu punch to Joe's face took five weeks to heal.

As he continued to strut through the mall, he could see them now, judging him, questioning his manhood. Sometimes they would go wide-eyed for a second before becoming self-conscious and looking away. Bart knew he didn't pass as a woman. Life had blessed him with an extremely masculine physique. The aforementioned chiselled jawline and shoulders wide enough that some doors were a problem. Hands so large and powerful they could crush walnuts. His bald head. At first, Bart had been upset when he discovered his receding hairline. His glorious golden locks had been the envy of many, not to mention easily transformed into several feminine stylings, and the word receding had an unmanly retreating kind of quality to it. Then he discovered male pattern baldness is caused by testosterone killing off hair follicles. He was too much of a man to have hair. Embracing it, he began shaving his head. However, it did make the blonde wig on his head a necessity, and thinking about it made the itching on his scalp ten times worse. He dared not scratch his head and risk messing up the hairstyling he'd already spent far too long on. Then, of course, there was the voice. This was a point of particular concern as he approached the store that was the goal of this little excursion to the mall. Once inside, he would have to talk, and he wasn't looking forward to it. Bart had a very manly voice. Not only was it incredibly deep, but it also had a quality to it that could only be described as authoritative. One time Bart had said hello to a group of passing off-duty soldiers, and they had all instinctively stood to attention and saluted. Any attempt he made at a feminine sounding voice made him sound like a teenager whose voice was breaking.

Bart entered the store, a high-end women's fashion clothing outlet. He stared longingly at the racks of dresses, blouses and skirts as he made his way to the counter. How he would love to spend the afternoon here trying on various things. He was too terrified to do that, though, and he didn't want to stretch out and ruin all the clothes he tried.

"Hi, how can I help you?" The saleswoman at the register greeted Bart, not missing a beat for a second or seeming at all put off by the fact the person in front of them was clearly a man in a dress and makeup. Bart was always impressed by people in retail. They were so good at pretending to be always happy and cheery that even if they really were put off by Bart's appearance, it never showed. What Bart didn't know was that this employee had just spent twenty minutes cleaning up after a customer had spilled their extra-large slushie over a clothing rack, and then a further twenty minutes explaining that they couldn't refund them for the slushie as they hadn't sold it to them. Retail workers deal with the worst of humanity every day.[19] A nervous man in a dress is a fairly relaxing transaction for them.

"Uh yes," Bart cringed at his attempt at a feminine voice. "I was just here to pick up my click and collect order?" He handed over his phone, showing the email receipt. Bart wasn't as smart as the other Dregs, he couldn't set up complicated PO box schemes, but the development of click and collect ordering was a godsend for people like him who didn't want to explain to their wives why women's clothing was being delivered to their house. And Rosalind needed to be kept from this at all costs.

---

[19] I have never worked in retail, but when researching this aspect of the book, all I ever got from former retail workers were the thousand-yard stares of war veterans.

Rosalind was the feminine yin to his manly yang.[20] She cared as much about appearing like society's ideal picture of a woman as Bart did about his manly reputation. An extensive reading list of women's magazines made sure she was abreast of the latest trends. One word from these hallowed texts, and she would burn entire sections of her wardrobe. Pants, flats, dry skin, body fat: all were dirty words for Rosalind. Hair anywhere but in long locks on her head had to be purged immediately. She complemented Bart perfectly, and he loved her to bits. But he knew her idealised worldview had no place for a crossdressing husband. So he covered it up. Some would call it dishonest, but Bart felt it was what Rosalind would want. It was what she did with all the other unwanted realities she had to deal with. Wrinkles, blemishes, her original hair colour: all constantly hidden from view. And anyway, more importantly, he had to keep it from the Dregs. How would it look if the manliest Dreg turned out to be a giant sissy? It would destroy the group. He couldn't do that to them.

The saleswoman returned with his order. "Here it is. Let me just check it's all here."

Bart didn't like standing still when out for this long. He could feel the eyes of people on the back of his head, wondering if they were questioning his right to be in this shop.

"One 'love me tenderly' minidress, one 'hot Italian nights' bralette…" The list only got more feminine from there, and Bart nodded politely as she read the list. He swore they didn't sound quite so girly when he was buying them online. "Okay then, would you like it gift wrapped?"

"Oh, no thanks."

"Are you sure? It's free?"

---

[20] I said yang, please stop giggling.

"No, I'd just like to—"

"Well, at least let me put it in a nice bag." The attendant carefully folded each item as she delicately placed them into the bag. Bart could only stand there and drum his fingers menacingly on the counter. God, his feet were killing him. He shouldn't have gone for the five-inch heels, but they just matched everything else so damn well.

"Okay, let's see…" She started typing on the sales terminal. "Are you a member of our rewards program?"

"No."

"Would you like to—'

"No thanks, can I just—"

"Are you a member of our loyalty club?"

"How is that any different from the rewards program?"

"Well, you see—"

"Actually, I don't care. Can I just pay and go?"

"Sure." The saleswoman scanned the barcode of the dress. "Huh?" She tried again without success. "Hey Katie." She called over another employee, and they looked confused together at the terminal. Bart could feel everyone staring at him. Felt their eyes on his skin. He wanted to scratch his face but he knew that would ruin the makeup. Eventually, they managed to scan the item. "Sorry about that. Is that cash or—"

"Card," said Bart as he hurriedly pulled his credit card out of his purse and waved it over the scanner. Thankfully it made a successful dinging noise fairly quickly.

"Let me give you your receipt," she said, holding the bag just out of Bart's reach. Bart's eyes were almost popping out of his sockets as he watched the reams of paper slowly make their way out of the register. After an eternity, it finished. "Here you go."

"Thanks!" said Bart and quickly turned and clacked out of the store, only now realising it was completely empty.

Once he was moving again, he felt better. As much as it scared him sometimes, he did enjoy being out dressed like this. Sometimes sales staff would compliment his choice of nail colour or his dress. Deep down, Bart knew they were just trying to make a sale, but it thrilled him to be treated like a real woman every time. Bart considered doing some browsing through some other stores, but his feet were killing him, so he thought it was time to get back to the car.

"Oh shit," said Bart to himself as he exited the mall. Between him and his car was a man stumbling seemingly randomly around the car park, occasionally swearing at a passerby or just to himself – it was hard to tell. Even at this distance, he could smell the alcohol coming off him. Bart attempted to discreetly walk around the man to his car but failed.

"What are you, some sort of fuckin' tranny?" the man spat at him.

Bart had parked in one of the more secluded parts of the mall's car park, mainly so he couldn't be disturbed while he gathered the courage to get out of the car. In retrospect, that had been a bad idea. Just ignore him, he thought.

Unfortunately, Bart had the man's attention. "What kind of faggot dresses like that?"

Bart sighed and thought, of course, the only person in town off his face at eleven in the morning finds his way to where I parked. What Bart didn't know was that this spot in the car park was completely downhill from the local pub, a near-perfect topographic catching point for inebriated individuals. The police usually rounded up whoever was left at six in the morning each day to stop it getting overcrowded.

He tried to get his keys out of his purse so he could just get out of there. This wasn't easy with long fake fingernails. Trying to get the keys out of his purse was like trying to manipulate one of those claw machines at an arcade. While he fumbled around with his purse, the man continued to approach. "Fuckin' ignore me, you sissy cunt."

"Listen, buddy, unless you want one of these stilettos through your forehead I'd back off, okay?"

"Ha-har," said the intoxicated man. "Fuckin' sissy, think you could take me?" the man staggered closer.

"Look, would you just fuck off mate?" said Bart as he gently pushed the man backwards. Unfortunately for him, Bart's forearm was still a force to be reckoned with. The man stumbled backwards, lost his footing and slipped. His head impacted the concrete guttering hard, and out of it seeped a liquid that rather perfectly matched Bart's nail polish.

"Ah, shit," was all Bart could manage.

CHAPTER 2

Damn Luddites, thought Tim as he tried to make out the directions he'd hastily written down over the phone. How hard was it to send him something he could put into DätaCorp Maps?[21] As he took the next turn, there was a brief feeling of deja vu, but it quickly dissipated when Tim got distracted by the matter at hand: a murder in Pax Gardens. This was what every cop dreamed of. Well, they didn't actively hope someone would get murdered. Okay, maybe there were one or two people Tim hoped would be murdered. The point was every cop dreamed of working a murder case. It was the peak of crime. It was the excitement he needed to distract himself from any remaining crossdressing desires, which was useful right now as these directions seemed to be taking him fairly close to the national park where his shame was buried. So close, in fact, that if he took the next right like the hand-scrawled note told him to, he would be entering the national park. That couldn't be right.

He saw a cop car parked in front of the dirt road into the park as he approached. The officer recognised him and

---

[21] DätaCorp Maps is similar to Apple Maps, except it sometimes accidentally kills people by directing them over missing bridges or roads that don't exist. Actually, it's exactly like Apple Maps.

waved him through. Tim started to get a feeling of dread in the pit of his stomach. He checked the directions again. It said to drive until he arrived in a familiar-sounding clearing. This had to be a joke, right? The Dregs were known for their extraordinary pranking skills, so it was entirely possible that they had recruited the entire police department into some crazy scheme.[22] However, that would still imply that someone knew he had been hiding evidence in the middle of the night at this remote location. Joke or no-joke, this situation was no laughing matter. A few minutes later, he arrived at the clearing. It was crisscrossed in blue and white police tape. Several police vehicles were already at the scene. Crime scene units were walking around in full protective forensic gear. The place wasn't nearly as calm as it had been the other night when it had just been him and the stars. He knew he shouldn't have trusted those damn stars. An area to one side had become the de facto car park, so Tim parked and walked over to Sergeant Mills. "Took your fuckin' time," she said. She was in one of her better moods.

Tim thought Sergeant Mills must have been named that way because she was very coarse and good at grinding people down over time. "Well, I don't work well with directions," he replied.

"Could've used you to help set up a perimeter. Press should have caught wind of this by now."

"The press?"

"Yeah. We're not entirely sure of what this is all about, but there's been some weird shit going down."

"Weird shit?" asked Tim, trying to stop his voice wavering.

---

[22] As a result of said pranks, several Dregs may be missing organs, and all are still banned from entering the Vatican.

"Come over here and take a look." She started walking off towards a grouping of police cars and people. What worried Tim was that she was walking exactly to where he had dug a rather shallow grave a week or so before. What did she mean by weird shit? Weird shit as in a mutilated corpse or weird shit as in "We found your secret stash of women's clothing, you freak"?

They passed a few officers who were putting up more tape, even though the entire field had been encircled three times already. They were hoping no one would ask them to do something difficult like collect evidence or patrol something. Tim waved hello, and they reciprocated with minimal effort, then went back to chatting and spooling tape. Were they staring at him? Tim looked back over his shoulder. They were chatting about him, weren't they? The fuckers knew, didn't they? Mills was going to take him over there and show him the bag of clothes and say, "Recognise these?" Then the Dregs would pop out and take a photo or something. He really wished he'd bought his gun with him. Actually, he'd lost it a few months ago at the pub, but so far, no one seemed to have asked about it.[23]

Mills led him under another pointless layer of police tape as they approached what seemed to be the focus of everyone's attention. Tim tried to think of some excuses for the clothes. They were the result of a failed bachelor party,[24] an ill-conceived gift for Julia, he had been sent the wrong order

---

[23] I'm just going to state now that we never actually see the gun again in the plot. My editor complained that I'm literally going against the narrative principle of Chekhov's gun here, as well as figuratively in several other places. Instead of fixing it I'm just going to ruin the suspense so you won't be disappointed when it doesn't come up again.

[24] The Dregs considered a bachelor party a failure if it did not include at least one of each of the following: strippers, arrests and broken bones.

by mistake and the store's confusing returns policy ended up with him accidentally burying it in the middle of the bush.

They reached the circle of crime scene investigators. Tim didn't want to look down, but the sergeant gestured with her coffee. "Take a look at this."

Tim slowly looked down and saw his expertly dug grave with a dead body lying in it. Oh, thank god, thought Tim, it's not a duffle bag, just a dead body. Wait, what?

He thought he'd better say something and managed a confused sounding, "Umm, okay."

"A dead body isn't interesting to you?"

"Well, yes, but you said it would be weird. It looks like a pretty standard body to me." What it did not look like was a bag of women's clothing. Did clothing transmogrify into human beings when buried for long enough? No, that was insane. At least Tim hoped it was as he didn't need the other dozen or so graves around here rising up right now. What he did need was a beer. God, how he needed a beer.

Mills handed him a manila folder with some grainy photos in it. "This is from a security camera at Pax Gardens Central Mall. The other day someone noticed a dry bloodstain in the car park. They checked their security camera footage and found this."

Tim looked at the pictures, they seemed to show a woman shoving a man over and then carrying the body away.

"Didn't pick them up leaving the car park but the victim in the picture matched a local regular at the tavern who hadn't been seen in a few days. So we tracked his phone here."

Oh good, thought Tim, it's just your run-of-the-mill unpremeditated murder and an unfortunate coincidence. Tim relaxed a bit, but still, he did wonder where the bag was. And another thing bothered him. "Didn't you say this was weird?"

"I'm getting to that. See the suspect there?" she tapped the photo.

"Yeah."

"That's a man."

Familiar feelings of dread and panic filled Tim. "What?"

"We asked around the mall if anyone could remember anything weird that morning. Several witnesses confirmed there was a crossdresser in the mall around the time of that footage, wearing that dress and acting paranoid. Image forensics confirmed it, based on all the available data: that is a man."

A murderer happening to borrow his shallow grave for a body could be excused as a coincidence, but this? Tim fought against the instincts that told him to start running as fast as possible and tried his best to look like a man whose world wasn't threatening to collapse around him. Amazingly, he pulled it off, and Mills said, "Still don't think it's weird, huh?"

"Well, no," lied Tim. "I mean, I'm sure there's lots of crossdressers out there, and there's lots of people capable of murder out there. Logically there must be some overlap."

"Okay, got one last thing to show you. This way," said Mills and walked off again.

Tim guessed what it would be. Obviously, the bag of clothes must have gone somewhere, and they'd found it. Probably for the best really, thought Tim, it would be nice to know where it went. They walked into a temporary tent that forensics had set up, and Tim was surprised to find it didn't contain the bag from the grave currently inhabited by a corpse. It did, however, contain the other sixteen bags Tim had buried in the general vicinity.

"Shit," he accidentally said out loud.

"Finally weird enough for ya?" said Mills.

"Yeah," Tim added noncommittally as he watched several forensics experts examine clothing items from one of his duffle bags before shoving them into zip lock evidence bags.

"There were multiple tyre tracks from different vehicles parking here so we wondered if maybe they were a repeat offender. We searched the area and found all this. Sixteen separate sites scattered around here. Thought they'd be other victims, but it's all just…" Mills paused and picked up a zip lock bag containing a blouse before emitting a confused sounding "…clothes."

"Well," one forensics officer who was examining a miniskirt interjected, "I'd say fashion was a victim. I mean, look at this cheap, tacky shit, I wouldn't be caught dead in this." The officer went back to cutting samples from the miniskirt for testing. Tim winced as she tore off a sample from one of his favourite skirts. It was one thing to criticise his fashion, but he wished she didn't have to take such glee in destroying it in front of him.

"With all this clothing," continued Mills, "we thought we'd find some trace of hair or skin or something with some DNA in it. But nothing. The whole lot's been scrubbed. All we're getting is traces of industrial solvents. This guy's a professional. Which made me think: Why make the rookie mistake of leaving his phone on? Why do it in broad daylight in front of a camera? He wanted us to find all this. It's some sort of weird ritual. Like all these other graves full of clothes represent future victims. I think we've got a serial killer on our hands."

"Nah," said the forensic officer, who had now moved on to dissecting a padded push-up bra that Tim had fond memories of. "There's a ritual to this alright, but I think you've got it wrong. I think he's already murdered sixteen people before.

The ritual is a reality inversion. He buries the clothes and wears the corpse Buffalo Bill style. Would explain why it's women's clothing. Anyway, this time, he just screwed up, accidentally buried the wrong bag. Must have been really annoyed when he got home and realised he left the corpse out here."

Tim sighed. Everyone who watched *Criminal Minds* or *CSI* seemed to forget that criminal profiling was completely useless in real crimes. "Maybe a national park is a convenient place to dump things, be it clothing or corpses, and two people choose the same secluded clearing to dispose of their stuff."

"So," said Mills, "it's all just a coincidence?"

"Yeah, maybe." Tim hoped so anyway.

"Nah, you know what they say. There's no such thing as coincidence when it comes to—"

But before Mills could finish, another officer entered the tent, "Sergeant, we've got our first press van trying to get in. We tried setting up more police tape, but they're just walking through it."

"Shit," she turned to Tim. "Look, we've got enough people here, I want you to head on down to the mall and help with getting witness statements. I'm going to go deal with the press," she said as she brought out her favourite truncheon.

Tim gladly accepted the invitation to get away from this place as fast as possible. He followed Mills out of the tent and made a break for his car. Once inside, his hands reached for his keys, but they were shaking uncontrollably. This was a nightmare. There were people literally going over his feminine clothes with a fine-tooth comb looking for the owner. The entire police force was looking for crossdressers. There were so many questions concerning the situation. By not telling them the bags were his, was he deliberately perverting the course of justice? He could go to jail for that. At the very least, he would get a fine for littering. And where the hell was the other bag? Did someone murder a person in drag just to bring the police to the remains of his adventures as Brooke? Was it the Dregs? It would be a pretty spectacular prank if it were them, thought Tim. He wouldn't even be mad. But he knew that none of the Dregs would dare taint their manliness by crossdressing, even for a prank. He laughed to himself at the thought of Bart trying to crossdress, and his hand stopped shaking long enough for him to start the car. If only, he thought.

⸎

Bart took a sip of the beer and stared at the problem. He still couldn't believe it. Of course, not much about that day seemed believable. Bundling a corpse into the boot of his car and driving off. Panicking— No, not panicking. Men didn't panic. They stayed calm and figured out how to dispose of their corpses. There was no straightforward way to get rid of a body. Fire was Bart's preferred disposal method for getting rid of inconvenient feminine things after a day as the Madam. Something about fire felt very masculine to Bart, but it wasn't a great way to get rid of a body in the middle of the day. Tossing it in a lake would mean sourcing some chains or cement blocks, and he didn't want to leave a corpse in the car park at Bunnings. Briefly, he considered some sort of dismembering option but really wanted to avoid getting any more blood on his dress. Then he remembered Tim mentioning serial killers burying their victims in remote bushland. It was his best option considering it was broad daylight. After driving around the bush for a while, he had found a nice spot that looked like a perfect place for a shallow grave.

He felt silly dragging a corpse around fully dressed up. People thought walking in heels was hard. Try carrying a corpse in them. Sure, he could have changed into the spare clothes he had in the backseat. But he had spent a lot of time getting made up like this, and he wasn't going to just let a little manslaughter ruin it. He was a man, and men didn't give up when things got tough. "Shit!" said Bart as he broke a nail on one of the first shovel-loads of dirt. After few minutes of digging, his shovel hit something. It was too soft to be a rock and too solid to be earth. He scraped away some soil and revealed some fabric. There was a handle, so he grabbed hold and dragged it out of the dirt.

Bart couldn't believe it: he'd broken another damn nail. Also, the bag buried exactly where he had decided to dig was equally unbelievable, and the mysterious bag was probably of greater concern right now. What could possibly be in there that someone would bury out here? Another corpse? Or maybe something valuable? Bart decided to be an optimist, despite everything else that had happened today, and went to unzip the bag. As he unzipped it, he expected piles of gold coins or stacks of cash would come pouring out, so he was quite shocked when masses of women's clothes burst out. "What the fuck?" he said out loud as he stumbled backwards. Unfortunately, one of his heels chose this moment to lose the fight against the masses of muscles it was holding up and snap off, causing Bart to fall even further backwards and land on the corpse.

Bart groaned as he realised he had ruined his heels, his dress and lost several more nails. Pulling himself up, he took another look at the grave. He hadn't imagined it. The bag was indeed full of women's clothing. Perusing a few of the items, he checked the sizes. They were consistent with either a tall woman with broad shoulders or an average-sized man. Heels the largest size you could possibly purchase. Breast forms. Bart recognised what this was. It was a crossdressing stash.

This was the very problem he was now staring down in his backyard. Keeping his gaze on the bag, he took another sip of his beer. It was one Tim had recommended. Apparently, it was a Bavarian-style lager that had been brewed from holy springs deep in the Alps with an ancient yeast culture over one thousand years old before finally being filtered through a Trappist monk's socks. Bart swished the liquid around his mouth, sampling the flavours before swallowing. "You can really taste the monk," he muttered to himself before refocusing on the problem at hand. There was only one explanation for the bag: he'd been set up. How could the very spot he chose to dig contain a crossdressing kit? The whole thing had been staged. They must have drugged that stupid man he accidentally killed and then set things up so that his only option was burying the body in that exact place. Bart didn't know why he'd taken the bag with him. Well, partly it was because he didn't want to have to dig another grave. But if this was a setup, the bag could be part of it. He couldn't risk leaving it where he found it. Especially not after that community watch meeting the other night.

The community hall was full of chatter. There was nothing like a murder to make attendance at the weekly neighbourhood watch meeting increase by two thousand per cent. Through the chatter, Bart could just make out Rosalind and Julia's conversation.

"I just can't believe something like this could happen in our cosy little suburb," said Rosalind.

"I know," agreed Julia.

"I mean crossdressing, what kind of degenerate would do that?"

"What? I thought you meant, you know, the murder."

"Well yes, obviously that's horrible," said Rosalind.

Bart wasn't surprised by his wife's stance on recent events; it was in line with her past behaviour. There was the time she voted no in the gay marriage vote because she felt, for some reason, that she couldn't explain but that definitely wasn't homophobia that people she had never met being happy was somehow a threat to her own marriage. She was pro-life because she couldn't process the idea of someone not wanting to have an adorable baby. Rosalind would say her stance on these issues was because of her proper Christian upbringing. She could never remember exactly what brand of Christianity she followed. However, she suspected it was Catholic as she did feel vaguely guilty a lot and enjoyed a good glass of red. But she told Bart it was all the same Jesus in the end, and it didn't really matter so long as she maintained her faith and used it to solve society's issues, such as this outbreak of crossdressing.

What made less sense to Bart was why Julia was friends with his wife. Tim told him Julia found it hard to make friends on a nurse's shift roster, and what Rosalind lacked in personality, she made up for with a flexible schedule. Julia didn't so much enjoy Rosalind's company as prefer it to being alone.

But Rosalind told Bart that they found something in each other that had made their friendship deeper: the shared trauma of being a partner of a Dreg. Nobody else could quite understand what it's like to be on first name terms with half the local police due to constantly being called in the middle of the night to bail out several Dregs after one of their misadventures. No one else knew what it was like to have to store industrial quantities of bleach in order to clean up after a Dreg hangover. Julia had worked in emergency at hospitals and still had seen far worse injuries in the aftermath of various Weekends of Manliness. Julia and Rosalind were each other's support network when faced with the madness of their partners. It gave them a bond that Rosalind claimed was deeper than that of the Dregs themselves. Bart of course wanted to dispute such a ridiculous notion, but Rosalind also had trouble making friends, and the more distractions Rosalind had, the more chances he had to indulge in certain habits. So he didn't argue.

"Murder," continued Rosalind. "You know, it's been around since the dawn of man. But all this gender nonsense, that's all new. Back in the twentieth century, everyone knew what gender they were. Now people are claiming all sorts of crazy things."

Before Julia could respond, a small middle-aged man approached the podium on stage. "Hi everyone, welcome to this week's meeting of the Pax Gardens neighbourhood watch. I see there's a lot more of you than usual. I guess those flyers I sent out must have done the trick." The man chuckled and cleaned his glasses. This attempt at humour was met with silence and a blank stare from the crowd. "Well, anyway, I know we're all concerned about the tragic murder of one of our beloved community members, James Cooper. An upstanding member of the community, he will be sorely missed. He was a kind and gentle soul who we all know wouldn't have done anything to provoke this." Several people in the crowd teared up. Bart was not one of them.

Bart was, in fact, thinking, "Are you fucking kidding me? That asshole attacked me!" He had to fight every impulse to jump on stage and deck the defenceless little man saying these things. He compromised and gave the speaker a death stare.

The man, unaware of how close he had come to being beaten within an inch of his life, continued. "We are lucky enough to have with us today Tim Taylor, one of the officers assigned to the police investigation, to tell us how the community can help catch this degenerate and stop something like this happening again." The crowd clapped and Tim walked up to the stage.

"Hi, umm, yes, well, as a neighbourhood watch, the best thing you can do is act as extra eyes and ears for the police. I have here an image of the suspect taken from security cameras at the crime scene." He held up a grainy-looking image of Bart. "If any of you see this person, contact the police immediately. Do not take any action yourself as he could be extremely dangerous." A hand shot up in the audience. "Umm, this isn't really a Q and A," said Tim.

"You said *he*," said Julia. "That picture's pretty blurry, and they are clearly in women's clothing. Why are you so sure?" She smirked slightly. Bart could tell she was enjoying the discomfort she was causing her partner.

"Well, our forensic image analysts have been over the tape. They studied the body language and shape, and it's consistent with a man. Also, you can see here the amateurish application of makeup and what looks like a cheap wig."

"Not to mention the terrible choice in fashion!" someone in the audience yelled out to a few laughs.

Bart clenched his fist so hard, it drew blood. They would pay for this, he told himself.

"Isn't that a little sexist? I mean, couldn't this just be a large-framed woman?" asked Julia.

"Ummm, I suppose—"

"And does it even matter? Maybe the murderer identifies as a woman, and all this talk of them as a crossdresser is just pushing them further to the outside of the community and make it more likely they'll murder again."

"I'm just relaying what the analysts told me. Anyway, regardless of their gender, this is what they look like. We have a pile of flyers here with their picture and what to do if you see them. Thank you." Tim rushed away from the podium before anyone could ask any more awkward questions.

"Urgh," muttered Rosalind and rolled her eyes. "You don't need to peddle your gender ideology here, you know."

"I just don't think it's right, judging people on whether they have a feminine figure or not."

"And embarrassing your poor long-suffering boyfriend like that. I honestly don't know how he puts up with you sometimes."

Bart saw Julia's mouth open to utter some inane feminist retort when the head of the neighbourhood watch once again took the podium. "Thank you, Tim. Now we have someone else who wanted a chance to speak." He put his glasses on and looked at his notes. "Mrs Gertrude Ladymore of the, uh"—he adjusted his glasses thinking he must have misread—"of the Coalition for Calmdressing." He looked at the crowd for reassurance but got none. An older woman in a formal dress that wouldn't look out of place in the fifties walked up on stage and took control of the podium.

"Thank you. I just wanted to say that I think everyone has made a mistake in thinking that the fact the killer is a crossdresser is a coincidence. Both the murder and the crossdressing are symptoms of a deranged mind. I warned you all this would happen when we started indoctrinating children with the far-left extremist gender agenda that they claim is sex education. I was laughed out of the parents and community meetings at Pax Gardens Public, but no one's laughing now. As the police, neighbourhood watch and the government of this country have failed to stop this, I am left with no choice but to take matters into my own hands. I'm calling on all like-minded people to join me in forming the Coalition for Calmdressing. Together, we can work to bring back order to gender in Pax Gardens and stop this maniac before he kills again, or worse, continues to break gender norms. Thank you," said Ladymore and walked off stage to the sounds of a few sporadic claps from the crowd.

"What a nutbag," said Julia.

"She's just saying what we're all thinking," said Rosalind. "I, for one, am going to join her coalition."

"What are you, nuts? She's crazy."

"I don't think she is. I mean, look at the evidence. Bart and I have a traditional marriage and neither one of us goes out murdering people."

"Tim and I aren't married. I work for a living, and we don't go around murdering people either."

"Are you sure about that? Tim could be the murderer for all we know."

They looked at Tim standing on stage. His tie was crooked, his shirt was untucked, and they could make out a stain on his pants even at this distance. "I don't think Tim has enough style to dress as a woman."

The meeting was called to a close, and the neighbourhood started to mingle. Tim came back to the group, and Bart reluctantly collected a flyer with the suspect's likeness plastered to it, "What a disgusting brute," said Rosalind, studying the picture. "You can tell from his Neanderthalic face that he's a born criminal degenerate."

"You can't tell that from a picture like this," said Bart.

"Sure you can. I'm a great judge of character," she said before walking off saying, "I'm going to get one of the Calmdressing flyers."

Bart looked at the photo of himself, before scrunching it up.

$$\sim$$

The bag had to go. Luckily, Bart was well prepared for disposing of women's clothing.

His backyard had a fire barrel. Its stated purpose was for entertaining, and yes, the Dregs had enjoyed a good many beers while seated around it, but it was really his incinerator. This was a much larger load than he was used to disposing of, so he'd brought extra supplies. He poured in several litres of petrol, and he also chucked in a bunch of firewood mixed with some leftover BBQ charcoal. He needed to make sure there wasn't a trace left. Unfortunately, the bag was larger in diameter than the fire barrel. But Bart was someone for whom the phrase "square peg, round hole" was a challenge rather than a problem. After an impressive display of strength that Bart lamented no one was around to witness, he managed to get the bag three-quarters of the way in, but it wouldn't budge any further. It was close enough to the fuel that it shouldn't matter, so Bart lent down to the small hole he had drilled in the side to enable ignition.

Before he could strike the match, his phone started vibrating in his pocket. Bart didn't recognise the number but he answered giving a hesitant, "Hello?"

An unfamiliar sultry feminine voice answered. "Hi there Bart, I have a quick question for you."

"Who is this?"

"Never mind about that, I just wanted to know if the Dregs discovered that one of their friends was secretly a crossdresser, what would they do?"

"What?" he yelled at the receiver before looking around in panic. "I don't know what the hell you're talking about! Who the fuck is this?"

"Sorry, I've got to go. Enjoy the rest of your night, Bart," said the woman before laughing, and the line went dead.

"What the fuck?" Bart said to the phone. It had to be whoever had framed him the other day at the mall. They were toying with him. But why call him now? Did they know he was destroying the evidence? Were they watching him? He frantically looked around his backyard for someone he could blame for all this and beat the crap out of, which was the way Bart typically dealt with his problems. But there was no one. Bart thought it was probably best to finish what he was here to do as quickly as possible and get inside. He lent back down to the hole in the drum and readied a match.

Unfortunately, Bart had never studied chemistry, so he was unaware that the amount of fuel he had added was in perfect ratio to the amount of oxygen remaining in the barrel for combustion. The bag also provided an airtight seal at the mouth of the barrel. Bart had also never studied ballistics.[25]

The moment the match was struck, he was blown back several metres. The bag was launched out of the barrel at an impressive speed, and he was only able to track it for a moment before it was a dot in the sky. He sat in shock on the grass for a few seconds and then dived under a tree in case the projectile bag landed on him . Several minutes passed

---

[25] Bart didn't own any guns as he didn't want anyone to think he was compensating for anything. This also explained his lack of sports cars or anything over a predetermined height that could appear phallic in nature.

and he heard and saw nothing. Bart wasn't sure how long he should wait, so he let another few minutes go by before he came out from under the tree. There was no sign of the bag. All he could do was shrug his shoulders. It wasn't exactly as he had planned, but the bag was no longer his problem. He picked up his beer from where the explosion had thrown it. Its contents had spilled out. Bart felt that was probably for the best and went inside to inspect the damage to his eyebrows.

⌒

Stan sat in the waiting room. He flipped through the women's fashion magazines on the coffee table in front of him until he noticed the woman across from him and settled on the safe choice of a two-year-old issue of *New Scientist*. The idea of a science magazine being in a place like this was laughable to him. He knew being here was probably a mistake, but desperate times call for desperate measures. Especially now that the entire suburb was looking for crossdressers, thanks to whoever murdered that poor man. He confirmed he already knew everything the magazine had to tell him about science, put the magazine back and examined the room.

He looked at the qualifications on the wall and scoffed at the Masters in Clinical Psychology made out to a Dr Fiona Viola. To Stan, that was worth about as much as a degree in Homeopathy, Astrology or worse: Arts.[26] Not that he cared much about her qualifications. Dr Viola has some of the worst reviews of the clinical psychologists in the Pax Gardens area

---

[26] Stan himself had a PhD on the topological applications of algebraic and analytical principles to manifolds in seven dimensions and the implications of the results on the standard model of physics and the theory of relativistic computing.

that he could find on DätaSearch.[27] People were constantly complaining about her bending clinical guidelines, being short with patients, and other potentially unethical behaviour. Stan needed someone who was willing to think outside of the usual therapist bullshit if his plan was going to work.

He turned his attention to the table in front of him. In the middle was some sort of fruit bowl that appeared to be stacked full of onions. He picked one up and examined it carefully.

"It's an ornamental onion," explained the woman sitting across from him in the waiting room. "They're all the rage now."

Before he could begin to question this, the head of a woman poked out of the door. "Hi, Stan, is it? Please come in." Stan quickly tried to place the onion back in the bowl but caused a small avalanche of onions.

"Uh, sorry," he said, grabbing as many as he could off the floor.

"It's fine. I'll clean them up later," she said in a reassuring tone that had clearly been perfected over many years' experience with annoying patients. Stan was led into a calm looking office painted in neutral shades. "Hi I'm Dr Viola. Please sit down. Can I get you tea, coffee, anything?"

"No thanks, I'd prefer to get down to business." Stan knew these niceties were mind games to get him to open up. He wasn't going to fall for that. The armchair he sat in was extremely comfortable, but he did his best to resist its softness. Some people might say that going into a therapy session with an adversarial mindset was missing the point, but Stan didn't think much of those people.

"Okay then, what can I do for you?"

---

[27] DätaSearch is similar to Google Search except it mostly returns ads and a bunch of AI generated junk results. Actually, it's exactly like Google Search.

"Well, to get straight to the point, I've been crossdressing, and I need to stop."

"I see." Dr Viola made a quick note on the pad she had in front of her. "Well, that's nothing to be ashamed—"

"It is. Anyway, I'm not here to talk about how I feel about it. I just need to do something about it."

"Do something about it?"

"Fix it."

"That's not really a healthy attitude."

"It's not an attitude. It's a fact."

Dr Viola sighed. Stan recognised the sigh as someone who'd dealt with a lot of difficult people that day and was over it. He heard that sigh a lot. "Well then, tell me, why do you crossdress?"

Stan groaned. If he knew why he did it, then he could solve it himself, but he thought he should say something. "I just get this urge, somewhere deep inside me. I can bury it for a while, but eventually, it builds up, and I end up having to give in, buy something girly and get dressed up. There's just something wrong with me."

Dr Viola's expression softened enough that Stan worried that maybe he had let too much slip. "Stan, there's nothing wrong with you. This is textbook suppression. You try to deny your feminine side, and so it inevitably forces its way to the surface in an uncontrollable manner."

"Yes, I know, I read the textbook," said Stan, his patronising tone causing Dr Fiola's expression to resume its rigidity. "I came here to find a way to fix it."

"Well, that's easy, sort of. First, you need to come to terms with it. You need to accept the fact that this is part of you and find a way to let it into your life in a controlled way. Find some ways to express your femininity that doesn't cause it to come out in an uncontrollable explosion of crossdressing."

Stan rolled his eyes, "I know it's a part of me, the same way a tumour is. I want to cut it out. I'm a patient who has a disease and needs treatment."

Stan saw Dr Viola guffaw briefly before she regained her composure. "That's really the wrong way to look at this. The only way you'll get better is if you learn to embrace it."

"Oh jeez, embrace it," laughed Stan, "That's why no one would ever consider you a real doctor."

"What?"

"You think if I walked into an emergency department having just lost an arm, they'd tell me just to cut off the other one and embrace my armless lifestyle?"

"That's a false analogy."

"What if a paedophile walked in here? Would you tell him it's not a problem?"

"That's different. That hurts people."

"So does mine. How do you think the Dregs will react to this? Not fucking well, I can tell you." Stan didn't really think the Dregs would ever hurt him. But he'd seen Bart's overly muscled limbs destroy many people. He didn't want to risk being on the receiving end.

"The Dregs?"

"That's what my friends and I call ourselves. Surely you've heard of us."

"Can't say I have."

"But our exploits are legen—"

"Nope, never."

"Not even the time we ended up on page three of the *Pax Gardens Times* for that fire we started in—"

"Doesn't ring any bells."

"Well, I guess you don't get out much then. Everyone else around here knows us."

"I talk to people in the community every day. It's literally my job."

Stan looked at her silently for a few seconds, "You know, you're not being very welcoming for a psychologist."

Dr Viola drummed her hands on her armchair and looked in deep thought for a few seconds. "Look, Stan, haven't you ever had something you've had bottled up inside you? Like feelings for a girl or something?"

"My interactions with women haven't generally gone very well."

"Well, something else like that, like being angry and punching a pillow or a burst of laughter at something hilarious. Didn't it feel good when you let it out?"

Stan thought on that for a few seconds, "Well, I was constipated once, and, yeah, it did feel pretty good to let that out."

"That's not real—"

"But there are pills for that," he interjected. "I just took some Gastro-Start and, well, problem solved. That's what I've been asking you to do."

"You think there's just some medication that makes you a completely normal cis-gendered male?"

"No, I know the brain isn't that simple," he said, once again reaching new levels of condescension in his tone. "I was thinking we could do some brain MRIs."

"That's really more of a neuroscience thing."

"I know," said Stan, who was getting tired of having to explain simple concepts to this person. "But they offer neither office hours nor a secrecy oath."

"An MRI can't, for lack of a better word, cure you anyway."

"No, but it could let us find the part of my brain that causes my crossdressing urges. Then I just need a deep brain implant to do some targeted electrotherapy, and I should be good to go."

Dr Viola gave Stan a worried look. "That sounds very dangerous."

"Yes, well, I'm sure they don't get many volunteers, so I figured they'd jump at the chance. I'd let them use me in some sort of crossdressing neuroscience study."

"You can't have a study with one person in it."

"Wow, I'm impressed," laughed Stan, "A psychologist with a basic understanding of statistics."

Stan could see Dr Viola was struggling to maintain a client-friendly composure. "Okay, you want a cure? Fine. I'm guessing there's a sexual component to this?"

"Sorta," mumbled Stan.

"Why don't we just prescribe you some testosterone blockers. Your libido will fall and, well, problem solved."

"The goal here is to be less feminine."

"Masculinity isn't about hormones. A reduced libido wouldn't make you any less of a man."

"Yes, well, err…." Stan mumbled and tried to think of a logical argument against this course of action.

"Ha!" laughed Dr Viola, "I actually give you a way out of your predicament, and you won't do it on the tiny chance it might mess with your dick. Brain implants, that's fine, but not being able to get hard from a slight breeze, that's too far."

"Well, if you're not going to offer any real solutions, I'll take my business elsewhere," said Stan and folded his arms petulantly.

"Real solutions? So somewhere between brain surgery and hormones? There's plenty of batshit crazy psychology out there when it comes to trying to 'fix' people like you.

Everything from conversion therapy to good old fashioned Pavlovian behavioural conditioning."

"How do pavlovas have anything to do with psychology?"

"No, it's named after Ivan Pavlov, who did experiments on training his dog. He would ring a bell whenever he fed his dog, so eventually, the dog would salivate when he rang the bell. What we in the business call a conditioned response."

"Behavioural conditioning?" Stan lent back in his chair, stroking his chin while he thought, "Actually, that's not a terrible idea."[28]

"Oh no, that's a really bad idea! You could really do some serious emotional dam—" Dr Viola stopped mid-sentence and shrugged. "You know what, fuck it. If it ends this session, I'm just glad I could help. Please just don't tell anyone you got that idea from me," she finished, giving her most sincere smile.

"Thanks, doc," said Stan getting up, "I take back everything I said about psychs, well, maybe some of the things I said. Well actually—"

"Please just leave," she said, massaging her forehead.

Stan left Dr Viola's office, amazed that he had gained something useful. How had he not thought of this before? His crossdressing was probably caused by some sort of unintentional conditioning of his subconscious during his childhood, programming feminine desires in him. Yet another thing he could blame his parents for.[29] All he had to do was deprogram himself.

Stan was, of course, an excellent programmer and had written plenty of code in his time. Most coders know that

---

[28] Stan had never watched or read *A Clockwork Orange* as he didn't care for fruit or antiquated technology.

[29] Other things Stan blamed his parents for: global warming, the rampant inequality in modern society and, of course, the death of his beloved childhood cat, Hilbert.

once you know one programming language, it's relatively easy to switch from one to another. The programming logic and algorithms you knew were the most important things a programmer had to learn, not the language itself. Therefore, reasoned Stan, it should be straightforward to learn whatever language his brain was programmed in.

The problem was he would need some baseline information on his brain in order to reverse engineer it, but he had an idea of how he could get it.

⁓

Joe watched Claire through the viewfinder. He was disappointed that she was wearing the same dress as the one she'd worn on their date. It didn't matter, though. He was already getting his dose of femininity. She might have expected him to follow her but the last thing she would expect is for him to do it disguised as a woman. That's why he was dressed in a rather lovely evening dress right now – not because he wanted to but because he had to. He'd borrowed the camera from the photography department at work. It had a decent zoom, so he could make out what was happening from his vantage point, a bar across the road. As he'd suspected, Claire had gone back to work immediately. She likely didn't see him as a threat, so there was no reason not to. The bar she and her target were in was the same one she'd suggested for their date. He figured it was his best bet for finding her. It had taken several nights camped out here, watching and waiting for her to appear. Eventually, she showed up with a date.

In hindsight, Joe wasn't happy with his performance with Claire the other morning. He shouldn't have let her emasculate him like that. It didn't fit with the self-image he'd painstakingly created. Sure, he let himself be feminised on occasion, but never emasculated. He decided to fight back. Marketing had gotten him into this mess, so marketing would get him out of it. He was going to counter-blackmail her. Claire had much more to lose, considering she was actually committing criminal offences. All he needed was proof. And in the marketing world, proof was a fairly flexible term.

Joe tried to get a better image of her date, but the focus was slightly off. Unfortunately, the model of camera he had chosen used touchscreen controls and was almost unusable given the long acrylic nails he had attached. He could just have forgone the nails, but without them, he wouldn't have felt, well, complete. Why dress up if you weren't fully committed to it? What was the point of choosing a dynamite dress, doing your hair and coordinating everything with the cutest possible pair of heels just to ruin it all with manly hands? The nails helped Joe fully envelop him in femininity, keep him in the moment. To maintain that illusion of womanhood as long as possible, not for everyone else but for himself. He wasn't doing this for fun, Joe reminded himself. It was a necessity.

The nail salon was pretty understanding. He told them he needed long nails for playing the guitar. Nail technicians were usually a bit dubious when he explained that he needed them shaped in a rather feminine oval shape with pink polish applied to further enhance his guitar playing. He first used the guitar excuse years ago to explain to the Dregs in high school why he grew his nails long. Joe had been using this excuse for well over a decade now, and so far, nobody had ever seen him in the same room as a guitar.[30]

---

[30] This was because, during some drunken pub karaoke, the Dregs heard what Joe's attempt at singing sounded like and decided they didn't really want to hear anything remotely musical from him again.

Eventually, he managed to get a fingerprint onto the screen, correct the focus settings and took a few good shots. Operation Counter-Blackmail Claire[31] was going perfectly, except maybe he should have gone a shade or two lighter on the nails. He took a moment to inspect them one more time, before going back to the viewfinder to find that Claire and her date had disappeared. Shit, he thought, he really needed to capture the actual blackmailing happening; otherwise, he was just some creep photographing a couple on a date. He crammed the camera into his purse and quickly made his way out of the bar. From his vantage point Joe had a clear view of the street to the left of the bar, so he could only assume they went right, and he immediately set off in that direction. His pursuit couldn't have been considered speedy as he struggled with his stilettos and cursed whoever thought faux cobblestones were a good idea. Turning a corner, there was no sight of them. He struggled to think of how he could have lost them.

"Looking for someone, Joe?" said a familiar voice behind him, "Or should I say, Josephine?"

Joe turned around and saw Claire standing in an alcove off the street, "Oh, hi Claire. Fancy seeing you in this part of town," he said in such a convincingly casual tone that most people would have denied him basic worker's rights.

"You've been a naughty girl, Joe. I explicitly told you not to do anything stupid, but here you are."

"I'm just out getting some dinner."

"You really didn't think I'd notice the rather butch looking woman with the large camera across the road?" Joe was more worried about being called butch than to have his plan

---

[31] You would think that working in marketing, Joe could come up with a better name for his operation, but he's useless without his focus groups.

crumbling around him. "Oh Jesus, don't look so hurt, Joe. If it's any consolation, I love the nail colour."

"Oh, thanks," Joe replied in a meek tone while trying to pull his dress down to cover his thighs more.

"The point is that trying some sort of stupid counter-blackmail won't work. You don't think I have friends in high places just for these sort of situations?"

"I don't think you're really the friendly type."

"Well, they're not so much friends as high ranking officials who I bribe or have a large amount of dirt on. You think I couldn't make anything you dig up on me disappear?"

"Fine, you win. I'll get your damn money."

"Oh, you don't get off that easily," said Claire in a more menacing tone, "I need to make sure you won't try and fuck with me again." She pulled a phone out. "Which one of your friends do you think would take the news that you're out in a rather lovely dress with your nails all done up the worst?"

"What?"

"I'd say Bart. He seems unhinged and strong enough that he might beat the crap out of you when he finds out, don't you think?" she started dialling.

"What are you doing? How do you have Bart's number? How do you even know Bart?"

"I did my research on you, remember? It's not hard to find pictures of the four of you all over Facebook in various drunken poses."

"You've made your point. Don't—"

"Whoops, my finger slipped, and it's dialling."

"Okay, I get it. You win just—"

Claire spoke to the receiver. "Hi there Bart, I just have a quick question for you." Joe just watched, horrified as she continued. "Never mind about that, I just wanted to know if the Dregs discovered one of their friends was secretly a crossdresser, what would they do?"

"Okay enough, I get it, please," Joe pleaded.

Claire agreed it was enough, "Sorry, I've got to go. Enjoy the rest of your night, Bart," she laughed as she hung up, "Oh, don't look so worried. I'm sure you can lie your way out of it if he asks about the phone call. You're good at that!"

"That was unnecessary!"

"Oh, I don't think so. I find sometimes people forget the grip you have on their balls unless you squeeze them once in a while." Claire squeezed her fist at Joe in a way that made his actual balls recede a little out of fear before she took on a much cheerier tone. "Now you be a good girl and run along. I need you to get all that money together for me." She started walking down the street before turning to say, "Oh and in case you were thinking of doing something far stupider than this, remember how this plan turned out."

Joe tried to think of some witty retort to all this but only managed "You bitch."

Claire laughed, "Oh, don't look so sad, Josephine. You'll look much more feminine if you—" Claire was cut off abruptly when a large duffle bag fell out of the sky onto her, snapping her neck instantly.

It took more than a few seconds for Joe's brain to process what he'd just witnessed. He stood there in stunned silence while his brain tried to make sense of it. It eventually decided: something horrible has occurred in front of us and we should panic. At which point Joe let out a scream and proceeded to panic. He went over to look at Claire. She was very obviously dead. Normal necks don't bend that way. But, given her history of deception, he decided it would be best to check this wasn't some sort of insane ruse.[32] A large, heavy bag falling out of the sky from apparently nowhere did seem like a strange thing to happen. He went to feel her pulse but recoiled when he remembered Tim telling him about forensics, and how stupid criminals are always touching bodies right after they murdered them. If only he had some of those latex gloves that crime scene investigators had, he thought, and then he had a second thought. He did have something made out of latex. They weren't really designed to be used as gloves, but they would have to do.

Joe pulled several condoms out of his purse. You might think it strange that Joe was carrying condoms in a purse used exclusively for crossdressing. But there had been several occasions in the past where sexy situations had presented themselves in unlikely scenarios, and his lack of protection had precluded his partaking in them. He had vowed never to be without them, no matter what the circumstance. There wasn't enough for all his fingers, so he decided to stick two fingers in each, which made him end up with crab-claw hands. He bent and checked for a pulse. There was nothing, which Joe was surprised to find was kind of a relief. He then turned his attention to the bag. Where the hell had it come from? Had it fallen from a plane? Or was this some sort of revenge from one of Claire's former victims? Part of him knew he should probably start running away from this as fast as possible, but the situation was so strange. He had to know what was inside the bag.[33] Getting a grip on the zipper was a struggle, the lubricant "for her pleasure" was making it difficult to get a hold. Joe decided in the future he should stop worrying about

---

[32] Many Dreg pranks had involved people faking their own deaths. As a result, Joe was desensitised so for him to have this sort of reaction, you know it must have been a brutal death.

[33] Joe should have known better than this as the last movie the Dregs had watched on their bi-monthly manly movie night was Se7en.

her pleasure and just buy practical things. Eventually, he got a hold of it, gave it a good tug and out poured piles of women's clothing. "What the fuck?" was all Joe could manage. Did whoever send this know about his crossdressing? Was this some double-level kind of blackmail where he is set up for the murder of his original blackmailer? Or was this some guerilla marketing campaign for a new line of women's fashion that had gone terribly wrong?

Whatever it was, Joe wanted no further part in it. It was time to leave. He took a few quick steps towards safety but then he remembered: she'd taken a photo of him! And she called Bart! Tim had told him many stories of the crazy things they had found on various suspects' phones. He couldn't just leave all that for the cops to find. So, he reluctantly walked back over to the corpse formerly known as Claire and sighed. She had fallen on her purse. She really had to be just as annoying a corpse as she was a person, didn't she? He really wasn't looking forward to touching her corpse again. Trying to minimise the corpse fondling was difficult as she was much heavier than she looked. He had to fully grasp her to flip her over, leaving her body with several lines of lubricant smeared across it, but thankfully also exposing the purse. After a quick pause to admire said purse, he grabbed the phone from it. Once again he was about to start running but realised Claire would have a lock on her phone. Most likely, it would need a fingerprint to unlock it. Great, he thought, more corpse fondling. After a frustrating amount of time spent trying to stretch out fingers, get them lubricant-free enough for the sensor to work, and figure out which finger she used, he was able to remove the lock from the phone.

Right, thought Joe, now we can get the hell out of here. He flung the condoms on the ground in one quick, fluid motion and started running as fast as his stilettos would allow.

CHAPTER 3

ell, at least I know what happened to the other bag now, thought Tim. Although the situation before him raised far more questions than it answered.

"I told you it was a serial killer," boasted Mills as she and Tim looked at the corpse. They were both watching a detective who was crouched over the body examining it.

Tim's response was delayed as another officer spooling crime scene tape politely squeezed between him and Mills as they set about making yet another perimeter. "It could be a copycat."

"The same exact brand of bag? The same brands of clothing inside? I don't think so." Mills looked over at the corpse again. "It is different though. I'll give you that."

"Really? A body being left in a busy public space is different to a shallow grave in the woods? Who would have thought."

The detective inspecting the body stood up and walked over to them. "Looks like the cause of death was a broken neck," he rubbed his beard stubble in an attempt to look like a proper hard-boiled detective. "The bag can't have been the murder weapon. It's way too big to wield it effectively for that. Must have been placed there afterwards."

"So it's some sort of ritual?" asked Mills.

"Yeah, I think the killer is showing their newfound confidence. They used to hide the bag, but now they're using it to mark their kills."

"Oh Jesus," said Tim, rolling his eyes.

"What?" said the detective, almost forgetting to keep his voice low and gritty.

"Everyone's a profiler nowadays. You know criminal profiling doesn't work, right? Just everyone's into it now thanks to that *Criminal Minds*, *CSI* shit."

"So, what, you think the bag was the murder weapon? Did it fall out of the sky and crush her?" laughed the detective.

"It's possible," said Tim, not sounding confident.

"This isn't fucking *Looney Toons* mate. Maybe leave the detective work to the professionals."

"I'll let you know when I find one," muttered Tim.

The detective looked ready to take a swing at Tim before Mills stepped in. "Alright, that's enough. Before you two try to kill each other, can we focus on stopping the person who is already killing people?" Tim and the detective nodded meekly like naughty schoolchildren. "Okay then, what else can you tell me? I'm guessing from the condoms he's moved on to sexual abuse too?"

"Well, that's the weird thing," said the detective, before remembering the situation in front of them. "Well, okay, one of the weird things. The forensic guys say there's no signs of sexual activity, but there is lubricant on her neck, her hands and her purse."

"So," said Mills before pausing and looking confused, "he rubbed his junk all over her but didn't go any further?"

"Something like that."

"And that took four condoms?" said Tim, a man who was reluctant to use even one condom during sex.

The detective shrugged, "Maybe he was really paranoid about physical contact."

"I thought this was a crossdresser, right? Isn't rubbing your dick over something a very masculine thing to do?" said Mills.

"I think he was marking his territory."

"He was trying to own this poor woman?"

"No," said the detective once again, rubbing his stubble and taking his voice down an octave, "he was trying to show that he owned her femininity. That it was his now. The bag's part of that symbolism too. He took her femininity and then killed her with it."

"I think that all sounds a bit silly," said Tim.

"Well, killing defenceless women isn't a smart thing to do at the best of times," the detective retorted as another officer walked over.

"Just talked to some bar owners down the street, said a crossdresser had been there a few nights in a row with a camera setup."

"Jesus, he was hunting, choosing his next victim, sick fucker. Did they get a good look at him?"

"Nothing we can use. They did say he had chosen a very nice colour for his nails."

"Well, I can see a bunch of security cameras around the street. One must have caught them. Check all of them between here and that bar."

It's fine, thought Tim. There just happened to be a crossdresser in the area when his bag of crossdressing supplies crushed a person. This is all just a coincidence. It had to be a coincidence because otherwise, someone was leaving him some sort of Dexter-style messages about their shared experience crossdressing through crime scenes, and that was insane. His hand started shaking again, so he quickly shoved it into his pocket. Unfortunately, he wasn't fast enough, and Mills noticed. "Tim, could I talk to you for a sec in private?" she led him under another layer of police tape, "Julia called me the other day. She says this case is stressing you out."

"What? Well yeah, of course, dealing with this kind of shit is stressful."

"She said you've been drinking a lot recently."

"Well, maybe I've had a few more beers than usual."

Mills sighed, "I think we're going to take you off the case."

"What? No, you can't do that!"

"I saw your hand just then. You're clearly not dealing with the stress well."

Tim was panicked but maybe getting thrown off the case wouldn't be the worst thing in the world. So far, there was nothing connecting him to the case and no real leads on the actual killer. Perhaps this would just go down in history as one of those strange unsolved strings of killings that would become a popular podcast in twenty or so years. On the other hand, the lab techs hadn't examined their latest bag discovery. The cleanup job had been a bit rushed as he was cutting it close to the end of Julia's shift. Could he be certain this one would also be clean? No, he'd have to keep an eye on things and, if necessary, steer the investigation away from himself. Tim figured that by this point, he'd already slightly perverted the course of justice so there was no real harm in going for full-on perversion.

"Please, Mills, this is the case of the century!" he pleaded. "This could make our careers. We could retire early and live off doing interviews for true crime podcasts! Please don't do this."

Mills sighed and thought for a few seconds, "Well, we can't have you goin' around twitching like that. You'll spook the witnesses."

Tim was about to suggest perhaps lunchtime beers at work might help calm his nerves but felt on a second pass at the idea that wouldn't help the situation.

"Maybe if you agree to see one of our support psychs to help you be a bit less of a headcase, I could make the case to keep you on the case."

"Sure, whatever it takes." Tim didn't really like the idea but preferred it to being taken off the case, not to mention going to prison.

"Good. I was already worried about you so I made you an appointment for later today." She handed him a card, "Take the afternoon off to get your head straight."

Tim looked at the card and offered an insincere thanks before he headed to his car.

"Oh and Tim," said Mills, making him pause in his tracks. "Maybe lay off the drink. Julia said she'd keep an eye on you for me, so don't think you can bullshit me."

"Sure, no problem," said Tim, smiling. Out of visual range, he got rid of the smile. No crossdressing, no beer. How was he expected to relieve tension? Joe would tell him to get laid, but Julia hadn't been in the mood since all the murder business had started. Without beer, he knew the thoughts would creep back. The inexplicable draw to womanhood would return. Weird feelings about gender would circulate in his head. Questions like "What's the harm in doing it one more time?" would continue until they reached "What if I could dress like this all the time?" Tim didn't want to know what could happen after that. It needed to be short-circuited well before that point.

Some would suggest talking to a psych about all of this was a good idea, but he needed to be here keeping an eye on things. Needed to make sure that nothing was done to that bag until he had a plan. Should have spilled his coffee on it, he only now thought, and said, "Whoops, guess it's contaminated with my DNA now, sorry," but it was too late for that. He sighed, got in his car, and drove towards his appointment.

∽

Tim looked at the depressing selection of magazines on the coffee table. The only one that wasn't out-of-date was this month's edition of *Cooking Weekly*, which had the feature article "Fifty fun and trendy recipes for onions!" The cover had an overly happy model eating an onion as if it were an apple. Tim was trying to make sense of it when he was called into the office.

"Hi Tim, have a seat," Dr Viola said as he entered, "Now, what is it I can help you with?"

"Oh, nothing really. I'm just doing this to keep my boss off my back."

"Ah well—"

"So I was thinking I could just pay for a full session, get a receipt and show it to my boss," he said as he pulled his wallet out.

"Well, your work is actually paying for this session so—"

"Great, you can just tick my name off, and I'll be off." Tim put his wallet away as he headed for the door.

"They requested I write a report on your mental fitness to continue as an officer."

Tim stopped in his tracks. "Ah."

"So why do you think they've sent you here?"

"I don't know, just a general check-up?" he said as he sat down.

"It says here it's because you're showing signs of stress and self-medicating with alcohol."

"Well yes." He waved his hand dismissively. "For some reason, they think being a bit stressed out after encountering several bodies killed in strange circumstances isn't normal."

"No one said it's not normal. I'm sure all your colleagues are finding it tough. They just want to make sure you're dealing with it in healthy ways."

Tim sighed. "I've already decided to cut back on the beers."

"Yes, and that's a good first step. Next, we need to look at if there's anything more we can do. We'll start by looking at the source of your anxieties. What do you think is particularly stressful about this?"

"Did I mention the dead bodies?"

"Yes, but—"

"Dead bodies are pretty stressful, even before you take into account the—" Tim suddenly realised what he was about to say and caught himself "—other stuff."

But Dr Viola narrowed her eyes, and Tim feared his pause had given him away. This was confirmed when she decided to press it. "What other stuff?"

"Oh, you know, all the strange stuff around the case. Bags of clothes turning up in strange places, strange condom rituals, crossdressing killers."

Unfortunately, Tim was a very bad poker player[34] and Dr Viola was easily able to pick up on his discomfort saying the

---

[34] Despite being awful at poker, Tim was the Dregs' best poker player and had won the inaugural Dreg Poker Championship. Stan was so obsessed with the mathematics and probabilities he couldn't bluff, Bart would get mad if he lost a big enough hand and flip the table, and Joe spent most of his time at the table trying to look cool while smoking a cigar with a glass of fine scotch while he bled chips.

C-word, "Do you find the fact that the killer is a crossdresser stressful?"

"What? No, I mean who cares." Tim cleared his throat. "They're obviously a deranged killer, so it's not surprising they're a weirdo freak in other ways too."

"You think crossdressers are freaks?"

"Well no. Yes. I don't know." Tim shuffled in discomfort in his seat. "I think we're getting off track here. I think we should be focusing on, you know, the crushed corpse I looked at this morning. I think that's a fairly traumatic thing to see. Or maybe we should do one of those inkblot things, and I can tell you how many of them remind me of a penis or my mother or both."

Dr Viola silently studied him before scribbling down a few notes. "I think the real problem here seems to be you have some hang-ups around gender. What exactly is it about a man pretending to be a woman that upsets you?"

Tim didn't like where this was going. "It doesn't upset me, it's just not a normal thing to do. Just like murdering people. Why don't we talk about that?"

"I'm not going to leave this topic until you tell me the truth."

Tim sighed and thought for a few seconds. "This is all confidential right? You can't tell anyone anything that I say here without my permission?"

"Yes. Even the report I give to your work won't mention any specific details, just give a broad outline of your mental state."

"Alright then." Tim took a deep breath. "I may, or may not, in the past, have engaged in crossdressing."

"I see. The past?"

"Well about—" Tim counted on his fingers "—nine days ago, but I've since given it up forever."

"Okay, and why do you think this is causing you distress?"

Tim thought it was best not to mention his bag of shame being used as a bludgeoning implement causing him to be a suspect in his own case, but luckily, he had plenty of other stressful things to talk about. "Well, I mean suddenly everyone in Pax Gardens is looking for crossdressers."

"So, you're worried about being discovered?"

"Obviously."

"There's nothing to be ashamed of. It's a perfectly normal thing to do. Our modern understanding of gender identity is that there's a whole range of—"

"Gender identity?" He laughed and shook his head, "I don't think we need to start bringing all that transgender stuff into this."

"Well, there's a range of different gender identities in the gender-diverse spectrum. I'm not saying you're trans, but perhaps you might be genderfluid or non-binary."

"I think you're getting carried away. I'm just a normal man who likes to dress up as a woman sometimes."

"Yes, that's what we in the psychological community call denial."

"No it isn't."

She sighed, "I think you need to come to terms with your identity. Maybe you could try talking to some people you trust, what we would call your support network. It might be easier to talk to them about this stuff than me."

"So your suggestion to me is to come out as a crossdresser at the exact time everyone is demonising crossdressing?"

"Well, I didn't say publicly, but if the public were to see one of their own police officers is one of these gender-diverse people they're currently afraid of, maybe that would help calm their fears."

"Or it would make them afraid of the police and start vigilantism and mob justice. Anyway, it's not the public I'm afraid of. It's the Dregs."

Dr Viola almost dropped her notepad. "Did you say Dregs?"

"Oh, you've heard of us?" Tim perked up at the thought of their infamy spreading. "We are pretty notorious."

"We?" said Dr Viola, trying to hide her shock, "So you're one of these Dregs then?"

"Yep."

Dr Viola was lost for words for a few seconds as she tried to process this. Eventually, she recomposed herself. "And you've never discussed crossdressing with them? None of the others ever shown any signs they'd be up for it?"

"What are you nuts? Of course not. They're all real men. Unlike me, they'd never touch this stuff."

"I think maybe they would be more understanding than you would think."

"Listen, you may be an expert in psychology, but I know the Dregs far better than you."

"I don't know about that," Dr Viola muttered to herself.

"What was that?"

"Sorry, mumbling. I was saying maybe we should change the topic," said Dr Viola before flipping through some of her notes, "Your work says they're concerned about your drinking. How much have you been having?"

"Oh, you know, the usual amount."

"And what's the usual amount?"

Tim tried to stay vague. "A few a night."

"Every night? That sounds a bit excessive."

"Yes, well, I told you I'd cut back."

"But not of your own choice. Do you think a couple a night is a healthy amount?"

"I think so. I mean, zero is obviously the healthiest amount, but that's a boring life, isn't it? You have to find a balance."

"But that's the behaviour of someone experiencing addiction, Tim. They have a particular amount they need to get their high."

"Well, that's not me. I'm not drinking for the alcohol. I'm doing it for the taste. Beer is just a hobby to me."

"A hobby?"

"Do you have any idea how many craft beer breweries there are nowadays? I'm pretty sure if we walked outside, there'd be at least one opening up within a block of here. Probably more. There's just so much to sample. There's your lagers, pilsners, stouts, hefeweizens, saisons, dunkels, porters, kolchs, goses, and that's before we even get to the ale family. Red ales, brown ales, pretty much most of the colour spectrum nowadays. Dark ales, white ales, fifty fucking shades of ales. And then, of course, there is the behemoth that is the pale ale family. India pale ales, Australian pale ales, American pale ales. There are over one hundred and ninety countries on this planet right now, and I guarantee you everyone has their own fucking style of pale ale. There is so much beautiful, delicious beer out there and every day I'm not sampling it, a brewery is closing down, and I'll never get to try their triple hopped India pale ale. Right now, there's probably the only crate of some amazing brown ale from a small craft brewery in Chile being unloaded at a port destined for some small specialty hipster bottle shop in Melbourne that I could be missing out on because I'm here talking to you. I'm just a hobbyist who cares about his craft. If I was into painting and liked experimenting with colours, would you think I had a problem? Would you accuse me of getting high off the paint fumes?"

Dr Viola underlined the word "defensive" on her notepad. "The difference, Tim, is that painters would consider the fumes to be a bad thing, they would try and limit their exposure, maybe wear a protective mask."

"I didn't say alcohol was a good thing."

"Still, most hobbyists can moderate themselves. People who play sports will take time out to rest muscles and joints. All I'm saying is you need to moderate it."

"And as I've already told you, several times, I've already cut back." Tim didn't say it out loud, but his cutting back attempts so far had consisted of having a 7.5% double IPA instead of the 9% triple IPA he'd originally planned. Also, since he'd made such a sacrifice, he thought he should reward himself with an extra can.

Dr Viola lent back in her chair. "So, you're stressed because work is intersecting with your secretive lifestyle and engaging in your 'hobby' helps you relieve your stress. Is that a basic summary of the problem?"

"I suppose."

"Well, it sounds like you've got things backwards. You're using alcohol to control your crossdressing when really I'd recommend using crossdressing to control your alcohol," Tim wasn't overly enthusiastic at the suggestion. "Please just consider it, Tim."

Tim sighed, "Fine, I'll consider it."

"Thank you." Dr Viola looked at her watch. "Well, we're out of time. So, for now, I'll recommend that you're fit for duty so long as you take steps to reduce your alcohol intake. I'd strongly recommend dealing with your gender issues as part of that, but I don't want to force you to do anything you're not comfortable with."

"Thanks," said Tim as he got up and walked out of the office. Dr Viola sat down to write her notes for that appointment.

She paused when she got to the part of her notepad where a single word was underlined: Dregs. She stared at it for a while before shaking her head. "It's just a weird coincidence," she told herself.

Tim stepped out into the street. That could have gone better, he thought, but at least it would satisfy Mills for the time being. To cut back on the beers, he needed to reduce his stress, and there was only one way to do that: make this murder case go away, or at the very least, make the parts that were connected to him go away. Then he could cut back on the drinks until work got off his back about things. Eventually, the murderer would be caught, or their thirst for blood would be quenched, and everything would go back to normal.

First things first: he had to get rid of that bag. It was the most likely piece of evidence that would lead back to him. Getting it out of evidence without being seen would be tricky, the place was obviously crawling with cameras, but he had an idea.

Stan stared at the avocado for several seconds before glancing over to the laptop screen and scribbling the pressure and flow rate reading it displayed onto a notepad. In one smooth motion, the avocado was swapped out for an onion, and once again, Stan stared at it intensely. He glanced back to the laptop and almost dropped the notepad in shock. The display showed the blood flow rate had ticked up a couple of cubic centimetres per second, more than a statistically significant amount. Stan couldn't believe it. Onions really were more attractive. He felt that had to be an entirely false statement, but he had the empirical evidence. He couldn't argue with it. There was a sudden urge to test and rank all the fruits and vegetables in his apartment by sexual attractiveness, and he almost got out of the chair before reminding himself he had work to do.

He was sitting naked in a dining chair except for the experimental phallometer strapped to his groin. A series of straps held the laptop-sized device between his legs, and a rat's nest of cables streamed off it to a series of power transformers, liquid nitrogen canisters and his laptop. Another series of cables emanated from a strap on his left arm, a worrying number of them connecting to the series of power transformers. Stan wasn't sure how safe this all was. The faint smell of ozone coming from his crotch was a little concerning, but he had calculated that the power input into the laser array was too low to burn the skin. Worst case, there might be a little mild sterilisation. Then again, Stan hated children, so that wouldn't be such a terrible thing.[35] Besides, getting the phallometer had been less than trivial, so he had to try it at least once. Of course, the only phallometers in the city were the ones that Stan was to be tested with by DätaCorp. So how do you steal a piece of expensive high-tech equipment from a mega-corporation whose entire business is basically surveillance? It turns out it's a lot simpler than you would expect. Of all the people in the world, the ones who knew exactly how intrusive and Orwellian DätaCorp's technology could be were the DätaCorp engineers building it. So they made sure none of it was installed in their labs. Once you were inside DätaCorp, you were in the one place they couldn't look, their black spot. Of course, there were security guards, but they were well aware they were somewhere near the top

---

[35] In fact, all the Dregs had unknowingly already spawned several Dreglets due to an unfortunate incident one weekend of manliness involving a crate of blue label scotch, a game of truth or dare and a sperm bank.

of the list of jobs that DätaCorp was trying to automate. This resulted in a lack of company loyalty combined with the need to gather emergency funds. Stan slipped them a fifty after hours, walked right into the biometrics lab and gained himself the shiny prototype phallometer currently gently heating his genitals. The most difficult part of the whole operation for Stan had been getting the fifty-dollar bill. He had long since evolved beyond the need for physical currency and had forgotten how it worked. He spent a long time trying to figure out what blockchain he needed to authenticate the transaction against before the guard told him he just handed him the physical token and there was no verification, much to Stan's horror.

But that was done, and now that he had the phallometer, he could begin his deprogramming. He had his baseline data, readouts from looking at various inanimate objects. He was surprised at his arousal levels at the small floral arrangement in his kitchen and had flagged it for further study. But for now, he had to focus, and, unfortunately, the next task was testing the negative reinforcement mechanism. He took a deep breath as his hand hovered over a large red button he had set up on the table. He pressed it, which caused a rather large voltage of electricity to flow through the band strapped to his upper arm. "Motherfucking, shit, cunt!" yelled Stan, deciding it was definitely not something he wanted to do again, which was exactly the point. The negative reinforcement was deemed negative enough, so Stan typed a few commands into the laptop, making it so that now the electric current would activate automatically if the phallometer went over 600 strecks[36] from the baseline.

---

[36] Strecks are a form of angular measurement primarily used for directing artillery fire. Stan thought it would be appropriate.

Stan would have preferred some sort of positive reinforcement, but it was impractical to constantly reward himself for not being aroused. Not to mention being aroused let off a cocktail of endorphins, so his positive reinforcement would be competing with his body's natural reinforcement. No, it had to be negative reinforcement. To make things easier, he'd thought of some other negative methods. One idea was to associate femininity with something wholly flacidifying, perhaps displaying a picture of his grandparents naked each time he felt an attraction to crossdressing. But this raised too many impracticalities: how would he get the photo? His grandparents would never agree, and even if they were willing, how would he explain why he needed it? He would most likely need to develop a cover story of a new photography hobby over several months before even broaching the subject of nude portraits with them. He didn't have time for that. And in the end, pain was more effective. It made sense to fight one of his body's natural impulses with another one. Stan really hated pain. His bathroom cabinet had more opiates in it than the combined stash of the heroin dealers who lived in the apartment upstairs. Even the word scared Stan. Pain, it had that horrible 'ain' ending that sounded as if something was being drilled into some part of you.

It was time to get started. Stan reached into a container next to him, pulled out a lipstick, unfurled it, put it on the table, and stared intently at it. It was mere fractions of a second before the phallometer measured a jump from a flaccid 100 strecks to an impressive 1000. Immediately the current began to flow through Stan, and he let out a series of curses. Unfortunately, the curses didn't stop the pain, and it was at this point Stan realised he forgot to program a cooldown time. He managed to get his right arm up and bat the lipstick out of the way, and luckily, it took only a few seconds for the phallometer to record a more acceptable reading, and the pain stopped. Stan slumped back on his chair, panting and sweating before cursing his oversight and fixing the code.

He took a deep breath, pulled a pair of heels out of the container and put them in his eye line. Of course, the phallometer was immediately off the scale, and the electricity flowed, although for a much more reasonable time in this instance. Stan groaned and took the heels down. The data on the laptop screen showed things were far worse than he thought. This might take a while, he thought, as he braced himself and took a pink pair of panties out of the box.

∽

Joe examined the row of taps in front of him and sighed. He would just get whatever looked half decent but could feel Tim's voice in his head saying: "You only get one beer before your palate is ruined, so it has to be the best one."

He looked to others ordering their own drinks for perhaps some guidance, but they were all getting various cocktails themed on sci-fi shows like a Cantina Martini, a Gallifreyan Heart-Stopper or a Pan-Galactic Gargle Blaster. Others were drinking champagne from Chateau Picard.[37]

This was Pax Gardens geek bar. It started out eighties themed when you entered, but this illusion quickly collapsed when you noticed the Nintendo 64 play corner and the recently cleared out area for the virtual reality headset where patrons could sit in a virtual bar and experience virtual social

---

[37] The vineyard owners were not trying to make a sci-fi themed wine and were actually just called Picard. They had no idea why their wine had suddenly become so much more popular.

anxiety. Joe got back to the task at hand and went back over the taps. "What the hell is a troll ale?" he asked the bartender.

"Ah, that's a new limited edition we've got in," the bartender explained as if he was selling a trading card. "Someone took the website 4Chan, ran it through a machine learning algorithm to make a chatbot and asked the chatbot how to brew beer. This is the result."

"Can I have a sample?"

The bartender poured a sample into a cup that was designed to look exactly like the kind Whoopi Goldburg served drinks in on The Enterprise D, but not one customer had ever noticed. Joe swished it around in his mouth. "Huh, you can really taste the rage stemming from deep inadequacy." The echo of Tim in his head was satisfied. "I'll have a pint."

At this point, you are probably wondering why Joe is in a bar by himself. Or you may have realised there is only ever one reason why Joe is in a bar by himself. But on this occasion, he had a specific purpose.

Claire's death, while gruesome, was in some ways fortuitous. His blackmailer was gone. However, Claire had put measures in place to make sure she was as big a pain in the ass in death as she had been in life: the dead man's switch. Without Claire around there was no one to disable the system she had set up which would email everyone he knew, destroying his hard-earned personal image. Luckily, Joe had stumbled onto a potential solution: the phone. He had grabbed it because he knew he needed to make sure he wasn't linked to Claire in any way. But her email inbox contained enough information that he now at least knew the email account that the automated system appeared to be ready to fire from. Claire was smart enough not to leave any passwords lying around, so he was stuck. Usually, at this point, he would ask for Stan's help. Stan had previously assisted in removing certain compromising pictures from the face of the earth and launching one or two minor cyberattacks against women who couldn't understand the one-night part of a one-night stand. But Stan was the kind of person who asked questions, questions Joe wasn't confident he would be able to lie his way through. So he was at this bar to procure a Stan substitute. There weren't many problems that Joe couldn't fix by picking up the right woman. Often, they seemed perfectly happy to trade their services for his goods. Of course, such behaviour risked him being labelled as a prostitute but, luckily for Joe, he was a man, and such comparisons were unlikely. And on the off chance someone did make the comparison, Joe had a lengthy speech he could launch at a moment's notice about prejudice against sex workers and the stigma they have to put up with.

The last time Joe had been in this bar, when the Dregs had made the regrettable decision to let Stan choose their after-work drinks location, Joe had picked up a cybersecurity analyst. Most of the people in this bar were so awkward that picking up was almost trivial for Joe. He'd felt like a wolf in a pack of sheep. Even that description implied effort on the part of the hunter. It was more like a whale in a field of plankton.[38] The point was that this place had the skillset he needed. Now it was time for interviews.

Normally this would be fun for Joe. He could examine the intricate feminine details of each candidate, maybe spot some new clothes he might purchase, see a new shade of eyeshadow he liked, or a hairstyle he might emulate with a wig. But the

---

[38] It should be noted that whales have not had a great time in the modern era and if things continue this way, plankton will probably outlive them. No metaphor for toxic masculinity there.

women in this bar weren't what Joe usually looked for. The first candidate was a train wreck. Joe could see the places where the lipstick ever so slightly left the boundaries of the lip. The curl job on her eyelashes was amateurish, and the eyeliner a mess. Joe couldn't understand women like this. They had the benefit of a feminine figure, breasts and a hairless female face, things he could only dream of, and they didn't even appreciate it. Poor fashion choices, little to no makeup. Pants of all things. Joe gritted his teeth through his usual routine until he found out they were a graphic designer and moved on to a rising YouTube star to an escape room attendant to a comic bookstore owner to a biomolecular scientist. There was another whose masculine boots irritated Joe so much, he gave up before even finding out their career.

Eventually, he decided that if he had to sit through one more conversation with some unmanicured, poorly blended excuse for a woman, he was going to give up. Downing another troll ale, he decided to give it one last shot before going home and getting dressed up so he could show all these so-called women how it was done. At the bar, was a candidate who looked like she may have brushed her hair within the last week.

"And what is it that you do for a living when you are not in fine establishments such as this," Joe asked, after an appropriate amount of small talk. At one point, he asked her name and was around eighty per cent sure she said it was Karen. Joe briefly thought that maybe he should be better with his dates' names. After all, if he'd remembered Claire's name, he could have avoided this whole mess. But that would be admitting Claire was right about his womaniser ways being a character flaw, and he wouldn't give her that satisfaction, even beyond the grave. Anyway, he thought, if they wanted him to remember their name, they should be better at marketing it.

"Oh, I'm a penetration tester," the woman replied before taking a sip from her appletini, "It's not as phallic as it sounds," she added once she spotted the smirk on Joe's face.

"If it doesn't involve phalluses, what does it involve?"

"It's a cybersecurity thing." Joe's eyebrow involuntarily lifted. "Basically trying to penetrate a network's defences."

"So, hacking?"

"Sort of. We do it to help businesses improve their network security. We call it ethical hacking."

Joe's face lit up at such ingenious marketing, "Oh, I like that: ethical hacking. Does adding ethical to a title work on anything morally dubious? This raises a lot of possibilities. I could start an ethical embezzlement company."[39]

The girl who was probably Karen let out a laugh and Joe decided to pretend that what he said wasn't meant to be serious.

Having found someone suitable, Joe let out all the stops. He used all his best jokes, subtly injected all his best compliments and flexed all his best muscles. Within a half-hour, she agreed to come back to his place. Not his best time but respectable enough that he would add it to the spreadsheet after he was done with her.

They burst through the door into Joe's apartment, wrapped in a passionate embrace while tongues darted in and out of various facial orifices. Seizing upon a moment when there was only one tongue in his mouth, Joe said, "You know what would be hot?"

"What?" said maybe Kate as she took the opportunity to take a few breaths of much-needed oxygen.

---

[39] Joe was unaware this already existed and is called the banking industry.

"Well, you know how earlier you mentioned the phallic associations of penetration testing?"

"Mmmm?" she moaned, giving a flirtatious smile.

"I'd love to see a demonstration."

"Ohh, so you like women to take control, huh? I can work with that. I guess I could hack into your smart TV and bring up a list of all the porn you've been watching and shame you for it."

"No, I had something else in mind," said Joe, simultaneously thinking it was time to clean his browser history. "You see, I'm being blackmailed."

"Really? Like ethical blackmail?"

"No, just the regular kind. I have this email address I know they're using, and I was wondering if you could do anything about it?"

"Oh, so you're just a poor defenceless man who needs me to spank all the mean bullies?"

"Wow, you're really into the femdom stuff, huh?"

The woman with an outside chance of being Kirsten could only nod enthusiastically as she pulled her laptop from her bag.

"Okay, well, the wifi password is—"

"I don't need it."

Joe could only pace apprehensively as he watched his date type manically. Text flowed down the screen in multiple console windows until she eventually called him over.

"What have you got?"

"So, I was able to get the address you gave me to bounce back some poorly formatted emails I sent, so that way I could read the SMTP headers and figure out its IP address."

"And what does that mean for me?"

"That IP address is a DätaCorp server. Whoever this blackmailer is, they must be using a DätaCorp Cloud Services[40] instance to run their operation. I'm not touching that."

"What? Why not?"

"You don't spend twenty years as a mega-corporation stealing most of the world's personal information without learning a little bit about how to stop people doing the same thing to you. That server is going to be locked down tighter than I'm going to tie you to that bed."

"Shit."

"Yes, well, now that the foreplay's done," she said as she pulled him towards his bed, smiled and threw herself backwards into it.

It was at that moment when Joe realised the position that definitely-not-Sarah had fallen into looked exactly like Claire's sprawled corpse as he had desperately searched for the phone, his condom-encrusted hands fawning over her as blood seeped from her face and flowed down to the sidewalk. Joe suddenly couldn't breathe. It felt as if someone was standing on his chest. He found himself slowly collapsing to the ground, gasping for air.

"Jesus, are you okay?" his date said as she rushed over. "I think you just had a panic attack. Have you never gotten this far with a woman before?"

Joe wanted to tell her how insultingly inaccurate that was but didn't have enough air for that.

"Are you okay? Should I call someone?"

---

[40] DätaCorp's Cloud Services are similar to Amazon's Web Services, except that with DätaCorp's version, you are supporting a horrible IT giant that is facing numerous allegations that it treats its employees like dirt. Actually, it's exactly like Amazon Web Services.

He managed to inhale enough to say the equally inaccurate statement, "I'm fine."

"Well, okay, if you're okay, I think I'm just going to go." She picked up her bag and backed towards the door. "The hacking was fun, but the whole panic attack thing is a bit of a turn-off, so bye!" she said as she slipped out.

Joe managed to pick himself up off the floor and sat on his bed. This was an unmitigated disaster. He was no closer to stopping the dead man's switch, and his main stress relief now appeared to induce panic attacks in him. Worst of all, panic attacks didn't market well. He decided he would call them temporary interruptions to normal breathing service. The words temporary and normal were much more calming than panic or attack. Joe decided at the next pitch meeting he would suggest a consulting package for the medical industry. Get rid of all these horrible words like syndrome and haemorrhage. Much better to tell a patient their brain's blood vessels underwent a spontaneous redesign. As fun as all this marketing was, he needed to refocus. He needed a new plan to stop Claire, but first, he needed to stop these temporary interruptions to normal breathing service.

How a dead woman was continuing to create new problems for him was inexplicable to Joe. He only knew of one way to solve problems: sleep with a woman who didn't cause the same reaction. That's how post-traumatic stress disorder works, doesn't it? Joe locked in this course of action before sitting down with a pen and paper to develop something that sounded better than post-traumatic stress disorder.

⁓

Stan was slumped in his chair, breathing heavily and drenched in sweat. The sweat did nothing but raise his conductivity, which made him decide to find a way to go back in time and murder whatever ancestor thought it was a good idea to evolve an endocrine system. The pace of his breath increased as he psyched himself up, clenched his left fist and grabbed the lipstick from the box. The moment he stared at it, he felt the familiar sensation of his arm being slowly destroyed for several seconds before it was mercifully stopped. Stan let out a whimper and a few tears before he checked his progress. It was an immense effort to pull himself forward in the chair, but he managed to use the table as support and made the painful journey of several inches to his laptop. He finally had enough data on lipstick to see if he had reduced the compulsion. The laptop took a few seconds to render the graph before showing Stan the horrible truth: the trend was in the wrong direction. He was getting more aroused each time.

Stan stared dumbly at the monitor for a few seconds, his eyes scanning for some sort of error before having a brief cry. How could he be getting worse? This made no sense, he thought, as he once again whacked the lipstick out of his sight and slammed his fist on the table. Unless, he thought, I am a masochist. Stan closed his eyes and thought of himself being naked and whipped by a dominatrix. The phallometer immediately detected statistically significant arousal and punished Stan for it. "God-fucking-damn it!" yelled Stan. He tore the wires from his arm and got out of the chair. "A whole fucking day wasted!"

He paced the living room with the phallometer and mess of wires still attached. This wasn't fair. From his vast knowledge of how the universe works Stan was aware that things generally were not fair, but he didn't enjoy being today's target of unfairness. All he'd ever wanted was fit in. He worked so hard at it with the Dregs. Months of forcing himself to drink beer and whisky before his taste buds adapted. Weeks of physiotherapy whenever a weekend of manliness involved sports. And now this one part of him, the only part of him holding him back from a normal life, wouldn't go away. Inside this crossdresser was a cisgender man waiting to come out. Stan stopped pacing and sat back in the chair, fighting back tears. "I just want to be fucking normal!" he yelled to the empty room.

Maybe it was some part of his identity that he couldn't change, something deep inside his core that couldn't be cut out without killing himself. Stan dwelled on this thought for a moment before realising that would mean admitting he was wrong about something and, even worse, admitting someone else, a pseudoscience-spraying psychologist of all things, was correct. That couldn't happen. No, there must be another solution. He'd spent too much time trying to reverse engineer himself and doing empirical analysis.

What was he thinking? He wasn't an experimental scientist. He was a theoretician! All he needed to do was come up with a theoretical basis for gender. Once he had that, he'd know exactly how to fix himself. Simple really. Sure, you could argue that people had been working on this for decades, and you could fill an entire library with gender theory. But they'd all been working in humanities and the arts. Stan wasn't surprised they hadn't figured it out. He always thought the arts should give up on this theory stuff and go back to do what they do best – make nice paintings or write the occasional sonnet. Give social science back to some actual scientists. Better yet, give political science back to some actual physical scientists and sort that whole mess out.[41] Stan decided to set

---

[41] People have tried this on several occasions, and it generally results in fascism.

his sights low and first fix humanity's issues around gender before attempting to douse the dumpster fire that was modern politics. He stood up with a new determination.

He set off to find a writing pad and pen to jot down some preliminary thoughts on an algebraic structure of gender but forgot his crotch was still wired in, tripped and face planted.

⌒

"Honestly, I think it's a bit of an overreaction," said Julia as Rosalind, Bart and she looked into the display window of upscale fashion outlet Travesti.

"It's a disgrace, right Bart?" said Rosalind.

Bart wasn't exactly sure what it was. It looked like a mix between a pantsuit and a leotard, so he offered a non-committal "Yes?" It didn't help that his focus was distracted by the neighbouring window full of more traditionally feminine clothing that he kept stealing glimpses of.

The strange clothing that the three were examining was, in fact, the centrepiece of a new androgynous clothing line for the store. The move had landed Travesti firmly into the crosshairs of the Coalition for Calmdressing, launching a wave of protests against them. Julia had protested against the use of the phrase "wave of protests" by the calmdressers. There had only been one protest, not a large enough oscillation to warrant the word. She suggested ripple.

Several coalition members had attempted protest banners and placards with phrases such as "Women's clothing for women!" and "We demand gender-distinct clothing!" as well as one poorly phrased sign that stated "Clothing should be sexually explicit!" Other protesters tried chants that weren't exactly catchy. "What do we want? Two genders! When do we want them? There have only ever been two genders, so we already have them!"

Of course, Rosalind had been the one who dragged them to the protest. Bart attended as her loving gender-normative husband. He tried to get the other Dregs to come along and support the cause, but they all had excuses. Joe's company was behind the marketing campaign for the clothing line and couldn't be seen protesting himself. However, he did explain that any publicity is good publicity and encouraged Julia to return to her rioting days and maybe set something on fire.

Bart would have been confused about why Julia was here, if he hadn't been getting frequent updates on her erratic behaviour from Tim. Ever since the neighbourhood watch meeting, she'd been researching crossdressing and transgenderism. She was always bugging Tim when they were trying to watch something on the couch together, showing him sad stories on her phone of trans people who had offed themselves and such. She said was going to stand up to all this calmdressing tomfoolery, and she'd stop Rosalind following them down the path to insanity. Bart didn't think best friends should try and undermine each other. In his opinion it wasn't very Dreg-like behaviour. But then again, as Bart would constantly remind people, he was a man with a masculine brain. Female friendships were not something he could, or should, understand. And anyway, he was quite fine with Julia trying to undermine this whole calmdressing thing. It would be one less thing for him to worry about if she succeeded.

As the group studied the clothing, Gertrude Ladymore walked up behind them, announcing her presence with an emotive outburst. "Ghastly, isn't it!"

"Mrs Ladymore!" gushed Rosalind.

"Please, dear, call me Gerty."

"It's great to finally meet you. I love what you've done with this protest."

"Yes, it's turning out well, isn't it? That's why I came over here. We're separating the men from the women. It's part of our effort to show that men and women are different, and there's no need for this disgusting clothing."

Julia laughed and put on her best impression of a posh voice. "Yes, women can't be seen in the company of a man in public, can we."

"Excuse me?"

"That's some very nineteenth-century thinking you've got there."

"And what do you have against the nineteenth century? It gave us modern marvels such as the railway and electricity."

"Yes, but there was, you know, the oppression of anyone who wasn't a straight, cisgender white man. Women couldn't work or vote or—"

"Exactly. Things have become more difficult for us. Working distracts from important work like making a family. And as for voting—" she scoffed at the word "—have you seen politicians these days? Brexit? That Trump fellow? What has voting ever done for us?"

Julia was about to protest further, but Rosalind sensed this and jumped in. "Bart honey, why don't you go join those nice men over there? I'm sure they'd love to hear your Dreg stories."

"Uhh, sure," said Bart as he reluctantly pulled himself away from the window full of women's fashion and walked towards the concentration of masculinity across the street.

"Now, I was just on my way to inspect the cake stall," said Ladymore, "Would you like to accompany me?"

"Oh, yes please," Rosalind gushed again.

"What kind of protest has a cake stall?" Bart faintly heard Julia's question as she followed.

Bart reluctantly walked towards the designated men's area of the protest. Rosalind had dragged him along, and he went as a dutiful husband should, but he had more pressing matters to attend to. The conspiracy that had framed him for murder knew no bounds. It seemed that they were now trying to make it look like he was a serial killer. They had somehow found the bag he had disposed of and used it to murder another person while dressed as a crossdresser. Then there was that menacing phone call. The call had scared the hell out of him, but then he remembered real men don't get scared. They take action. So he had dialled the number back the next day, ready to give his best attempt at a verbal beat down, but had gotten the voice mail message of someone named Claire, who for some reason included payment details in the recorded message. It wasn't until several days later he realised that the name was the same as the victim's.

The call was a setup to link him to the murder! It was clearly a well set up operation. But why target him? There were a lot of people who might have a grievance with Bart, people who had a dent in their skull with a shape that bore a remarkable resemblance to Bart's fists. But would any of them frame him for murder? Would any of them have the sophistication to pull off such an amazingly orchestrated conspiracy? There was also the possibility that this was a legendary Dreg prank, but the Dregs had never dared prank Bart. They knew how he reacted to surprises. On cold days Joe still complained about pain in the pins that were inserted in his thigh after Bart's surprise 25th birthday party. Without a suspect, Bart was at a loss. Secret conspiracies were ethereal things that he had no way of unleashing his rage upon. All he could do was prepare himself for whatever happened next, which turned out to be attending an anti-crossdressing rally.

Bart always felt nervous approaching other groups of guys, like he was cheating on the Dregs or something. Not that there were any homoerotic undertones in his relationship with any of the Dregs. Well, sometimes he wondered about Stan as he never saw him with any women and, of course, there was that one weekend of manliness that they had all agreed to never speak of again.[42] Not that there was any problem with being gay. These days, people were pretty accepting. Crossdressing, on the other hand, well, he was currently surrounded by people vehemently against it.

"Hi there, uh, fellow calmdressers," said Bart to the group.

The men were all in a loose semicircle staring at something being held in the centre and greeted his presence with a mumbled acknowledgement.

"What are you guys looking at?"

One of them turned around and said, "Sorry, but this is official Shooters, Fishers and Shooters party business," before turning back to their study.

Bart sighed but thought that Rosalind would expect him to make an effort. "We're all on the same team here, right? Can't I join in?"

The man turned around and studied Bart, "How do you feel about shooting, fishing and shooting?"

"I like at least two of those."

"Good enough," said the man and let Bart into the gathering. "Now see this protest. This is women's work. Strutting around, making noise, trying to get people to look at

---

[42] There were, in fact, several Weekends of Manliness they had agreed to never speak of again either because of large amounts of shame or because of the rules of *Fight Club*.

you. But men like us, men take action, we're not going to wait around for these useless police to do something."

"Sounds great," said Bart. "What are we doing here?"

"Hunting," he said and pulled up the grainy black and white photograph of Bart.

"Ah, I see."

"Those nanny state police bastards didn't want to give us any case details, so this is all we've got to go off."

"Wasn't there another security camera photo from the more recent murder?"

"Yeah, there was." The man pulled out another photo. "But you can see in the earlier picture that the crossdressing is far more amateurish. It's more likely he made a mistake the first time."

Bart was taken aback. Amateurish? How dare they! He was a seasoned crossdresser who had been on dozens of expeditions into the realms of femininity, and they had the balls to call him an amateur! Bart tensed his fist but managed to convince it not to launch itself at anyone yet. "I don't know," he said with uncharacteristic restraint. "He looks like a pretty convincing woman in the first photo."

The men all laughed. "Are you kidding? Look at the makeup. The brow line is all wrong, eyeliner very sloppy. The foundation is barely blended at the edges, and that's even before we even get to the trainwreck of a contouring and highlighting job they've done."

"Okay, maybe the makeup's not his best effort, but the rest of it is pretty convincing."

One of the men spat on the ground at hearing this. "Mate, you don't know what you're on about. Look at the colour of that dress. Very tacky. And those heels are so last season."

"Not to mention the horrible colour on the nails," added another of the group, to a general murmur of agreement.

Bart was furious but managed to hold back. He was in a strange position. He was used to defending his masculinity but this was the first time he'd had to defend his femininity, and surprisingly it stung far more. The idea that he couldn't pass as a woman, that he wasn't feminine enough, even when trying his hardest, hit him hard. What was stranger was how different it felt. Usually, his anger would come from his fear of not being manly enough. But this time the rage stemmed more from a well of sadness deep inside him. "You guys don't know what you're talking about! Look at the other photo. The first one has a way better sense of fashion."

The leader gave Bart a harsh look as if he was talking blasphemy. "That is a designer dress, and those shoes cost more than I make in a month.[43] He's clearly moved up in the world between the two pictures."

"And look at that nail colour," one member added, to which others let out a hum of implied jealousy.

"Simply breathtaking," said another .

"I'd do him," said yet another.

"You clearly don't know the first thing about hunting. You should go back over to the women and leave the men's business to us," said the leader of the group as the semicircle re-formed to exclude Bart and the hunters started discussing what brand of foundation their prey must have been using.

Bart knew Rosalind wouldn't want him to make a scene, so he resisted the urge to break back into the group and show how impressive his fashion knowledge was by beating the leader's face in and silently walked away.

---

[43] As the man was unemployed, this was actually a very small amount.

The bad news was that crazed vigilantes were hunting him. The good news was they were incompetent. But the idea impressed Bart. Why hadn't he thought of being a vigilante? It seemed like a very manly thing to do. Men didn't do things like ask for help or wait for other people to sort out their problems. They dealt with problems on their own, no matter how insurmountable. Bart always figured that on the Scott Expedition, the real reason Oates left the tent was not for some stupid noble sacrifice, but rather he was determined to walk off that ice sheet on his own without Scott slowing him down. If any further arguments in favour of this plan were needed, consider this. Batman is a vigilante, and it's hard to think of anything more manly than Batman. But most importantly, it presented a way out of this mess. There was now clearly someone killing people while crossdressing, possibly even on purpose. All Bart needed to do was find the killer before the police found a killer who may or may not be himself. Bart wasn't sure if any of that made sense, but it made about as much sense as his gender identity right now, so he was sticking with it.

After searching around for a bit, he eventually found Rosalind and Julia at the bake sale, still with that strange Ladymore woman.

"Gingerbread men?" said Julia as the three ladies looked at the cake stall.

"Yes, gingerbread men," replied the woman behind the counter with emphasis on the men, "Not gingerbread women. Those aren't a thing."

"Oh look, Bart, that's cute," said Rosalind as Bart walked over. "Those two melted together and look like they're holding hands."

"Oh, sorry," said the stall owner, and she disposed of the indecent gingerbread men, "Can't have that."

"Maybe if there were some gingerbread women, they wouldn't have to shack up with each other," suggested Julia.

The woman looked unimpressed at her, "Are you going to buy something or what?"

"Is this raising money for the cause?"

"It sure is!"

"Then no," Julia said, smiling at the stall owner.

"I'll buy one," said Rosalind. "Anything for the cause!"

"Great! Here you go! If you like it, we also do catering: birthdays, gender reveal parties, gender re-reveal parties."

"Re-reveal?"

"Oh, it's a wonderful initiative," explained Ladymore. "Many people were born before gender reveal parties were invented. Their families missed out on that wonderful celebration of traditional gender roles. Born again Christians have their baptisms later in life, so we thought, why can't born again calmdressers have their gender reveal parties later in life."

"Despite the fact that their gender would have been known to the world for decades," Julia pointed out.

"Yes, well, these days apparently people need to be reminded of it, otherwise, they get all kinds of strange notions."

"I think people have always had strange notions," said Julia. "It's just they were never allowed to express them before."

Bart could only stand there silently while the two argued, hoping that the expression on his face would not betray his own strange notions.

"Nonsense," retorted Ladymore. "I raised five kids, and none of them have any of these new-fangled ideas about gender and sexuality."

"How did you manage that?"

"Well, by making sure they have only the essential information about gender. They're taught from an early age that what goes on beneath their waist is none of their business."

"That's a bit extreme."

"Not at all," scoffed Ladymore. "I'm actually thinking of raising it to the belly button."

"But what about sex education?"

"They're all given sealed envelopes discussing the matter, which can be opened on their wedding night."[44]

Julia opened her mouth to respond to this new level of insanity but was cut off.

"Well, Rosalind, it was very nice to meet you, your husband and your…"—Ladymore looked Julia up and down—"…friend, but I must be off. I need to check that none of our supporters' clothing is breaching the Coalition for Calmdressing's morality code."

As Ladymore walked off, Rosalind groaned and rolled her eyes at Julia. "Why did you have to embarrass me like that?"

"Me embarrassing you?" laughed Julia. "This whole thing is an embarrassment!" she waved her hands in the direction of Ladymore, who was now measuring the length of a calmdresser's skirt with a tape measure, "Who cares if some guys want to wear dresses. You can't really be buying this can you?"

"People are dying, Julia. I try to be supportive of your causes. I baked cookies for your bake stall for refugees even though I don't think we should let them come here and take our jobs."

"But you don't have, or want, a job."

---

[44] All the letters said was: "We're very disappointed in your choice of husband/ wife as well as your decision to have sexual intercourse with them."

"Urgh, that's not the point," said Rosalind as she stormed off in a huff.

As Julia watched Rosalind chase after Ladymore, the sun was cut off by Bart's imposing figure. A good husband couldn't allow his wife to be treated that way.

"Now I'm fine with you trying to stop whatever the hell this is," said Bart, looking around. "But if you ever treat Rosalind like that again I'll make sure you spend the rest of your days helping Tim drink his meals through a straw."

The two death-stared each other. "Do you ever get sick of being a walking example of toxic masculinity, Bart?"

"Firstly, I'm not *an* example of masculinity; I am *the* example of masculinity. Secondly, there's nothing toxic about masculinity. if anything, it's…" he trawled his brain for whatever the opposite of toxic was. "It's harmless."

Julia looked at him.

He corrected himself, realising how placid that sounded. "I don't mean it's harmless masculinity. It's non-toxic masculinity. No, that's no good." He rubbed his chin in deep thought.

"Let me know when you figure it out." Julia smirked and walked off.

Damn it, thought Bart. He hated it when Julia made him look like an idiot. As a man, he could never hit a woman, so he deflected his rage to Tim.[45] He'd punch him in the arm later. He walked off towards Rosalind hoping to convince her to leave this terrible place so he could start his vigilante and/or Batman training.

---

[45] Bart had punched Tim's arm as a result of Julia humiliating Bart so often that it had developed into a hematoma. The second surgery finally convinced Bart to hit a little softer and alternate with other limbs.

CHAPTER 4

Of all the things about his life as a crossdresser, the ones that made the least sense to Stan were heels. They were quite possibly the silliest form of transport ever devised by man. Sure, the unicycle might be more impractical, the jetpack more deadly[46] and those bikes where you lie down to ride them more silly-looking. But heels had one feature that made Stan rate them lower than all of them: they were the only method of getting around that went slower downhill. Why throw away all that wonderful potential kinetic energy? The energy efficiency made Stan want to weep. But of all the inefficient devices of femininity, and there were a lot, he loved heels the most. They were the first thing he purchased for an outing as Loreta and the last thing he disposed of. It was hard to explain the attraction, the draw they held over him. Nothing felt as feminine to him as a pink pair of stilettos. Nothing felt as good when he slipped on a pair and strutted around the house. And nothing felt as satisfying as perfectly matching them to a dress. But he knew deep down they were not the optimally efficient shoe. As an engineer, he should hate them. But he loved them, and the contradiction enraged

---

[46] Before that particular Weekend of Manliness, there had been five Dregs.

him. The fact that he was wearing a rather boring pair of ballet flats made him a little sad. He was going a long distance with a heavy load, so it would be madness to wear heels. The part of Stan that loved heels argued that they were madness most of the time and several scars on his feet could confirm that, so why not wear them anyway? But his logical side had won out. So he trudged along the path by the river, hauling the phallometer-filled backpack over one shoulder in sensible shoes.

A reasonable person might ask what was so logical about walking along the river at two in the morning dressed as a woman with a stolen phallometer in tow? Stan was regretting stealing an expensive piece of equipment from a large corporation known for surveillance and tracking. His paranoia had been growing the past few days. Sure, maybe it had been easy to steal because he was a genius. Stan found most things in life easy because of his genius. Some would argue that it was because he was a white male from a well-off family with little to no hardship in his life, but Stan was fairly certain they were wrong. His genius explained his success in life and why everyone else was wrong, while the other theory only explained his success in life. Since his theory explained more, it must be right. But, he had to allow for the possibility that it had been easy for him to steal the phallometer because DätaCorp had the ability to track it. He'd wanted to crack it open and look for tracking devices, but the radiation warnings and mercury dripping from the device made him think twice. The simple solution was to get rid of it. Having it around reminded him of his failure and distracted him from the task at hand.

This was why he was taking the failed technology to his preferred location for disposing of evidence. Usually, he got rid of anything that could link him to crossdressing. This was the first time he'd disposed of evidence of a crime. The river was heavily polluted. The Dregs had experienced this first hand one weekend of manliness when they went skinny dipping and had peed blue for several weeks afterwards. Stan used the chemical exposure as an excuse to shave his legs and told everyone it was a side effect of the river. The strange thing was that shortly after that, all the other Dregs had reported the same symptoms and had lost leg, arm and even armpit hair. The chemical of cocktails, while worrying from an ethical, environmental and public health point of view, did make it a perfect place for disposing of inconvenient things. A few minutes in that river would dissolve clothing, wigs or even shoes. Stan paused to look at the river and sighed at the thought of all those heels dissolving below the water's surface. It would certainly cleanse the phallometer and possibly kill the poor DätaCorp technician sent to retrieve it.

None of this explained why he was dressed as a woman while doing all of this. The explanation for that was simple: when trying to avoid detection from a global mega surveillance corporation, it's best to wear a disguise, a good disguise at that. The only two roles Stan knew how to convincingly dress as were himself or a woman, and he wasn't that convincing as himself. He wasn't dressing this way for fun. This was a necessity. Also, according to the department of environment, the stretch of river in the middle of town was the most toxic. The place where shame dissolved fastest was there, and he wasn't going to walk through the middle of town undisguised carrying a stolen phallometer.

He trudged on for another few minutes before he got to the spot of maximum pollution. It conveniently coincided with one of the main bridges over the river, so he had cover while he worked. He plonked the bag down and started emptying it. Logically the items would dissolve faster if they were separated. Inside was the phallometer, along with several neatly arranged items of women's clothing, the runners up for tonight's outfit. He pulled out the pair of heels he'd been planning on wearing and sighed. As he actively contemplated switching shoes, his train of thought was interrupted by the loud thump of a large duffle bag falling out of thin air and landing several feet from where he was crouched.

"What the fuck?" he said to the heels before looking up. Above him was a woman leaning over the edge of the bridge before quickly disappearing. He looked around for other clues, but there was just him and more bags than before.

"The fuck?" he said to himself again. Looking upwards every second or so, he crept over to the new bag, grabbed it and moved back further under the cover of the bridge. Stan wasn't an idiot, a fact he spent a lot of time reminding people about, so he recognised this bag as the exact make and model described in various articles about a recent crushing death. He zipped it open, and it was indeed full of women's clothing. It appeared, Stan reasoned, that someone had just attempted to murder him and that someone may or may not have been a crossdressing serial killer.

This raised a lot of questions. Why was someone trying to kill him? Was it because he was a crossdresser? The last victim had been an actual woman, so that didn't make sense. They must have mistaken him for a real woman, a thought which sent a surge of pride through Stan before he remembered the whole attempted murder thing.

A crossdressing killer trying to kill a crossdresser? Too many coincidences. Stan didn't believe in coincidences. He paced back and forth under the bridge. Someone must have known he was coming here tonight. People don't just stand on bridges and wait to drop things on people. This isn't *Looney Tunes*.[47] But who would have known? His gaze fell onto the phallometer. Of course! DätaCorp knew he was coming here! But why would they want to kill him?

Stan started pacing again. DätaCorp weren't amateurs when it came to killing people. Their drone division kept landing military contracts for a reason. Yet, if they wanted him dead, he'd be dead. So either it wasn't DätaCorp, or they'd missed him on purpose. A flash of inspiration lit up Stan's face, and he paced faster. They missed on purpose! This was all part of the interview process! Google famously had interview brainteasers. It looked like DätaCorp has outdone them and produced full-on interview psychological warfare.

DätaCorp must know about his crossdressing. How? The answer was obvious: because they were DätaCorp. They knew everything. It didn't matter how many VPNs he used. They must have noticed his recent clothes-buying sprees. They must have set it all up, his theft of the phallometer, making sure a local murder appeared to be connected to crossdressing, making it look like someone had tried to kill him. All this just to see if he would crack. If they wanted to trick him into believing some crazy conspiracy about crossdressing killers, he'd outsmarted them and figured out the true conspiracy. With renewed energy, he hurled the phallometer and assorted pieces of evidence into the—for lack of a better word—water. He then picked up the duffle bag and headed downstream with a new determination.

～

---

[47] Or was it? Now that I think about it, two of the most common occurrences in *Looney Tunes* are things falling on people and crossdressing.

Once again, Joe sat at the bar. This time, he thought, *this time* he'd find someone. He'd been trawling bars the last few nights trying to pick up someone, anyone. But his game was off. Some suitably feminine girl would take an interest in him, and it would start out well enough, his opening line getting a good laugh. But he'd notice she had the same laugh as Claire, albeit with slightly less malice behind it, or applied the same shade of lip gloss, and the images of bones being crushed would return. He would miss punch lines, spill drinks and stutter. Eventually, the girl would go to the bathroom and never come back. Either they ditched him, or they had a very severe case of gastro. Neither helped Joe. Once he was close to sealing the deal when a nearby stool fell over, and the crash scared the hell out of him, causing a minor panic attack. The date stuck around out of pity, but Joe knew he was done. He was shaking so bad the martini in his hand kept losing its olive.

His poor form was beginning to be a problem. If he wasn't paying attention, he found himself considering the idea of getting his nails done or browsing women's clothing stores online. Luckily, so far, he'd caught himself before he got too carried away, but he was one lapse in concentration away from finding himself strutting down main street in his best stilettos. Even worse, he was distracted from sorting out the blackmail debacle. He needed release. He needed a close-up examination of raw femininity. As Joe sat there deciding which pair of his heels were, in fact, his best, he almost didn't notice the rather fine example of womanhood sidle up and take the stool beside him.

"Can I please get a glass of scotch, please? Something at least blue label. Straight up, no ice," Dr Viola asked the bartender.

Joe swivelled around on his stool before leaning on the bar to look extra smooth. "That's an interesting choice. Bad day?"

Dr Viola's drink arrived, and she quickly took a mouthful before closing her eyes in response to the sweet numbing relief. Eyes still closed, she replied, "Can you imagine a job where every day, people complain to you about their problems? Constantly?"

"Not really."

"Well then, consider yourself lucky," she said, opening her eyes to examine how much scotch she had left.

"Let me guess: doctor?"

"No, psychologist."

"Ah great." Joe put on one of his best smiles. "You'll love me then. I've got all kinds of interesting emotional problems."

There was an awkward pause as she examined him. "Really? That's your pick-up line?"

Joe shrugged. "Did it work?"

Dr Viola sighed and took another swig of her scotch, "Yeah, I guess."

The sex was slightly above average.[48]

"Ohhhh, I needed that," said Joe, almost out of breath as he untangled himself from the ropes and undid her handcuffs. He sunk back in the pillows and sighed.

"Hey," protested Dr Viola, rubbing her rope burns, "I'm meant to be the one using you as a stress relief."

"Sorry," said Joe as he let the endorphins envelop him. "I've had a lot on my mind lately."

"The emotional problems you mentioned?" she said as she leaned over the bedside table and refiled her tumbler of scotch.

---

[48] Average is also what my editor tells me my sales figures will be if I keep cutting out the sex scenes.

"Yes, those."

She poured another glass and handed it to Joe "Maybe, instead of trying to solve your problems with sex, you could try talking to someone."

"I'm talking to someone right now."

"No, you're not." She took a sip of her scotch and lay back down in bed. "I'm not on the clock."

"Probably for the best," said Joe before taking another sample of the scotch and nodding in approval. "If I told you too much about myself, you'd probably fall in love with me. Best to keep this superficial."

"How's that working out for you?"

"What?"

"Using humour as a defence mechanism?"

"Firstly, I was dead serious. Women stick to me like glad wrap's new super cling range," he said. He'd clearly spent too long on that marketing pitch. "Secondly, if anything, I use humour as an offence mechanism."

"Yeah, sure," laughed Dr Viola before enjoying some more of her drink.

"That sounded dangerously close to you trying to therapise me."

"Well, now I'm curious." She turned over in bed towards him and smiled. "What could a man as amazingly put together as you are possibly have to worry about?"

Joe didn't detect the sarcasm and thanked her for the compliment. He thought about it. Maybe it would be good to get a second opinion on everything that had been happening. His company hired consultants all the time. He wouldn't be getting therapy. He'd be hiring a lifestyle consultant. "Okay, let's just for a moment entertain the idea that I might be willing to talk to you about my problems. Why should I trust you?"

"Well, if you hired me officially, then legally, I wouldn't be able to tell anyone anything you said unless you were a threat to yourself or others."

"Okay," Joe leant over to grab his wallet from his bedside table. "How much for a session?"

"Two hundred," she said before quickly adding, "But this isn't payment for the sex, just therapy!"

"Jesus. Two hundred?" he stopped pawing through his wallet briefly to look at her, "That's way more than I would have paid for the sex."

He handed over two hundred-dollar bills. Most people these days don't use cash, let alone hundred-dollar notes. But for Joe, nothing made you seem richer to dates than flashing hundred-dollar bills. It showed you were so rich that anything less than a hundred was small change. It also showed you were so detached from the common man that you didn't know that no one uses cash anymore. Plastic money doesn't burn so he also had to carry around a few US bills to look cool while lighting a cigar.

"Okay, what's the problem?"

"I like to dress up as a woman."

Dr Viola sighed. "That's it? Nothing more interesting?"

Joe was slightly offended at being called uninteresting and almost told her about witnessing someone getting crushed to death, but thought it was best not to admit to disturbing a crime scene. "Oh yeah, totally uninteresting. Just, you know, would destroy my life if it came out. Who's going to listen to a marketing consultant who's a total weirdo?"

Dr Viola frowned and put on a more sympathetic tone. "You're not a weirdo."

"Yes, I am. My job is to know what people find appealing. Men who dress up as women do not test well. Statistically, I'm a weirdo."

"Well, they can't fire you for crossdressing."

"That's true. They even have a diversity and inclusion strategy now."

"That's great!"

"Not really," Joe took a sip of his drink, "I was on the committee that wrote it. I was in charge of fonts. You should have seen the one I commissioned for the project. Oh man, did it ooze equality. No one would look at that typeface and think anything but how included they felt by the words they defined."

Dr Viola felt something under the sheets before a look of disgust overtook her face, "Are you getting turned on thinking about it?"

"It was a really good font.[49]"

"Well, if they go to all that trouble to make an inclusive font, then they must be pretty accepting."

"Oh no," laughed Joe. "If anything, the font means they're not accepting."

"That doesn't make sense."

"You don't understand the marketing world," said Joe, putting on his best mansplaining voice as Dr Viola rolled her eyes. "You see, people are just as sexist and racist and biased as ever. It's just marketing that has advanced in the past few decades."

"That's a pretty cynical view."

"Is it? My firm has a diversity and inclusion strategy because it doesn't want to have to do anything itself. See, people have figured out that so long as you say you support women, disabled people, homosexuals, transgender people,

---

[49] While this book is almost entirely composed of fonts, unfortunately, we can't include Joe's font amongst our population of typefaces as it's fictional. If you want to picture it, imagine the exact opposite of Comic Sans.

you don't actually have to do anything. You've helped show society the errors of its ways, so now society can fix it while you continue to hire mostly straight white dudes. Basically, you're outsourcing diversity."

Dr Viola had finished her drink. This conversation would require more so she re-filled her glass. "Okay, maybe some corporations will make bullshit statements to cover up bad practices, but society has gotten better."

Joe laughed. "Has it? We used to make fun of people who would say, 'I'm not racist, I've got lots of black friends,' but now you don't even need ever to have met a black person to not be racist. You can say you voted for Obama. You've done your part to end racism, so now you can feel fine about locking the doors when a black person walks past your car. You support gay people because you voted yes in the marriage plebiscite. Not because you would go to a gay wedding – men kissing each other makes you uncomfortable. You can even just like your friend's post on Facebook where they've posted something supportive, slowly building your digital diversity support footprint, so if anyone ever calls you racist or transphobic, you can just pull out your phone and show them the proof."

"That might be some people, but most people do try to make things better."

"Really? People like you?"

"Yes," she said, offended. "I have several gender-diverse clients who I help with their problems."

"That doesn't count," said Joe dismissively. "You're paid for that. But when it comes down to it, you're still biased. How do you feel about our long-term dating prospects since you've learned my secret?"

"You really want to keep seeing me?"

"Well, no, but hypothetically."

"I'd be fine with it," she said, unconvincingly.

"Really? It's not a turn-off to think of me strutting around in a dress? Do you like the thought of me borrowing your makeup? Would you have come home with me if I'd been sitting at that bar dressed in heels and a skirt?"

Dr Viola sighed. "If I'm honest, probably not."

"Exactly. When it comes down to it, people haven't changed. They're as biased as ever. They've just learned to say the right thing. It's all words. Words in an amazing font."

Dr Viola thought over what Joe had said . Joe decided he'd won the argument and took a victory sip of his scotch. But then a look of horrifying realisation took over her face and she suddenly look right at him, "You wouldn't happen to be a part of a group called the Dregs, would you?"

"Oh, you've heard of us? Well, I'm not surprised. We are pretty notorious," said Joe, sounding more conceited than ever. "Which one of our adventures did you hear about? Was it the Dregs at the fireworks factory?"

"Oh for fucks sake!" yelled Dr Viola, throwing her arms up in frustration, "Would you just talk to your friends about this already!"

"What are you, nuts? If you've heard of us, you'll know that word Dreg is basically the definition of manliness."[50]

"Argh! This is insane! Why are you all so obsessed with this idea of masculinity? Can't you see how toxic it is? It's destroying you all!"

"You know, yelling at me isn't really a good way to convince me. If you'd studied marketing—"

---

[50] This definition was formalised in the first annual Dreg dictionary, written during one of Stan's more dull ideas for a Weekend of Manliness.

"Oh shut the fuck up!" it took all her restraint not to throw her glass at him, "You know where all you 'marketing' has gotten you? You're a lonely thirty-something male who's so afraid of being himself that you cling to the few friends you have that share your delusion about what being a man means."

Joe was taken aback. They sat quietly as he considered it, and Dr Viola managed to calm down slightly.

"Even if you're right about and the Dregs would be fine with it, you're still asking me to give up my spot in society and become something lower."

"Now that's transphobic," she stated bluntly.

"Is it? I'm not the one deciding this. It's society. They're the ones who view it as something less than a normal man."

"Considering them as not normal is also transphobic. You've had a privileged life for twenty-something years. You can afford to give up a little sliver of that."

"You know what my ancestors did to get me that privilege? You know how many genocides they were a part of? How much blood is on their hands? You're asking me to go up to them and say: hey, I appreciate everything you did to acquire this farmland by any means necessary so your descendants could have all the power, but I've decided to throw all that away, put on a dress and be shunned by society."

"I'm sorry, are you trying to make out the people perpetrating the genocide as the victims?"

Joe went to speak, but she cut him off. "Oh right, you're in marketing."

Joe could only smile at the mention of the word.

She sighed and said, "I can't believe I slept with you."

"Hey, where do you think you're going?" he protested as she got out of bed. I paid for the full hour." He could only watch with a mix of sadness and jealousy as she got dressed.

"I'm pretty sure my advice at the end of the hour would be the same as it is now: talk to your damn friends about this. I guarantee it won't go as you expect."

Joe thought over the idea for a few seconds. "I want a refund."

"Tough," she said as she grabbed her purse. "Good luck repressing all that, Joe. Enjoy your shallow existence." She exited the room before he could respond.

What a waste of time, thought Joe. Well, except maybe for the sex. It was obvious what had happened. He had fallen for her marketing. Believing that some stranger could say a few words and make all your problems go away. He should have known better. He'd been responsible for several ad campaigns for breweries that made the same claim. His ads were more honest. You did temporarily feel better after a drink or two.

Now he could focus and get back to the task at hand: stopping the ghost of Claire from ruining his life. He grabbed his phone and typed a quick email to his contact at DätaCorp asking for a meeting.

∽

If there was one thing Tim knew he could depend on, it was the incompetence of others. He thought this as he slipped in the back fire escape to the police station which, as usual, had been left propped open. This resulted from an under-the-table compromise between management and some of the smokers in the forensic division after an unfortunate chemical fire in one of the labs. The police station was surprisingly easy to break into, mainly because no one was stupid enough to try it.

It was two in the morning, a time when Tim knew none of the forensic techs would be around. He ducked down the hallway towards the lab but was momentarily distracted by a mirror in the hallway. He was disappointed with his eyeliner — nowhere near straight. And the tight leather mini skirt that had made him feel super feminine in his bedroom left him feeling a little exposed here. Why was he dressed as a woman? Not because he wanted to, definitely not. Not because nothing made him feel better than wearing the skirt he had on. Not because he loved doing his hair. Not because he felt some inexplicable draw to femininity. No, this was a necessity. While poorly defended, the station was covered in cameras. He couldn't simply walk in and reclaim his bag dressed as himself. It would take them two minutes to figure out where it had gone. But, Tim reasoned, if a crossdresser stole it, it would just look like the killer stole it back. Crossdressing happened to be the perfect disguise for this operation, and he selflessly spent several hours dressing up. To an outsider, he might have looked happy and enjoying preening himself, but if you'd asked him, he would have insisted it was all begrudged.

He couldn't just throw on any dress and put on some cheap supermarket lipstick. People expected the killer to be professional. He had to look the part. That's why the eyeliner was so frustrating, and definitely not because he wanted to look pretty.

Tim quickly checked his hair in the mirror and headed towards the lab. He would have fixed his makeup, but he knew that would only make it worse. Several days without beer meant it had taken a herculean effort to keep his hands still for the time it took him to look like this. And the constant sweating from lack of beer was doing terrible things to his complexion. But it would all be over soon. Once the case was closed, he could go back to beer, feel good for a change and be done with crossdressing forever. Sure, he had said this before, several times, but these were exceptional circumstances, and he was sure his life would never be exceptional again.

The problem with this plan, that he had only realised on the drive here, was that there was now another duffle bag's worth of crossdressing supplies to get rid of. If he kept generating as much evidence as he was destroying, he'd never be done with it. But there were more important things to worry about now, like getting the bag back and figuring out how to dispose of it.

The door to the forensics lab was also propped open. The lab techs, who rattled off impressive technical details of cases, could never remember the door code. The bag was in the centre of the lab, on a steel table awaiting dissection. It deserved better, thought Tim, as he fondly remembered that night as Brooke. Man, his outfit had been good. Tonight's had been a rush job. Maybe he could swap out a few items—no! Focus! This is not fun. This is a means to an end. The bag needs to go back in the hole it crawled out of. Grab it and get out of here before anyone investigates what is making the clopping sound coming from your shoes.

Getting out of the station was easy enough, but he wouldn't enjoy hauling the bag several blocks to where he had parked. He'd taken this precaution as he didn't want to risk traffic cameras picking up his car driving away from the police station. Walking out of the alleyway behind the station onto the street, he checked to make sure there were no witnesses before making the dash for his car. However, down the street a woman appeared to be watching him. This raised several pressing questions for Tim. Firstly, why is a woman walking around alone at two in the morning when a serial killer is on the loose? Secondly, and pressing enough that perhaps it should have been the first question, why does she have a rather large axe?

The woman took two rather menacing steps towards Tim, and his keen detective insights started turning over in his head. It was entirely possible that this woman might not be afraid of serial killers because she was, in fact, one. Tim was proud of this gem of criminal deduction as it conveniently explained the axe. As he stood there, full of professional pride at his detective skills, the possible serial killer started walking straight towards him. Tim decided now would be a good time to start running. Of course, this was easier said than done.

Knowing he would be carrying a rather large load, he hadn't gone all out with the heels and had opted for a reserved two-inch pair. However, he'd failed to take into account his skirt's shortness and tightness, which was severely restricting the angle that his legs could extend. As a result, he was not so much running as producing a series of fast but tiny steps. After an eternity, he made several metres of progress and turned back to check on his pursuer. For some reason, they hadn't made much of an effort to catch up. What a bitch, he thought, tormenting him like this. Well, he decided, he wasn't going to die like this. For starters, it would be too embarrassing. Not only was he crossdressing, but he wasn't even at his best. He wasn't going to die with his eyeliner in this state, not to mention the hatchet job he'd done on the contouring. Tim sighed and wished that his internal monologue had chosen a less axe-based description of his makeup.

He doubled his tiny pace, feeling the skirt strain against his thighs. After another few metres, he risked looking back. He seemed to have gained some distance, but the axe glinted in the moonlight, and he noticed blood smeared across it. Oh god, he thought as he faced forward again, she's already killed tonight!

Tim debated with himself whether that was a bad thing. Sure, murder was generally a bad thing, but maybe the killer had already satisfied their thirst for blood for the night and might give up on him. Or maybe the first murder had sent her into an unquenchable bloodlust that she would try to satisfy by any means necessary. While considering these arguments, Tim realised there was a new grinding sound coming from behind him. Taking another quick glance at his pursuer, it appeared that she was gaining on him and dragging the axe menacingly towards him. That settled it, it must be bloodlust. Once again, he tried to speed up, but his thighs could only take so much chafing. He couldn't believe he was going to die from a restrictive skirt and too light an application of baby powder. As the sounds of an axe being dragged along the pavement grew louder, Tim entered the bargaining stage of grief. He promised god, or whatever supposedly benevolent deity had caused this series of events, that if he lived through this, he would change. He would give up the drink for good. He would come clean with Julia and the Dregs about crossdressing. He'd even come clean with work about losing his gun. He really missed his gun now.

Then he noticed it. He was about to cross the bridge over the river! If he could get rid of the bag, he might be able to gain some speed. It wasn't perfect, but it was well known that the river was full of industrial waste. They might find the bag, but the chemicals in that water were far more powerful than anything Tim had access to. There wouldn't be a trace of him left on the bag. He ran – for lack of a better word – up to the side of the bridge and hurled the bag over.

Unfortunately, instead of a loud splash, there was a softer thud sound. Shit, thought Tim, as he realised he had forgotten the large section of bank before the actual river. He couldn't run down to the river like this, with a rampaging murderer right behind him. Hopefully, it landed somewhere out the way in some bush. He leant over the edge to see where it landed and was surprised to see a woman standing next to the bag looking a bit stunned and staring back at him.

Oh god, he thought as he pulled himself away from her sight, I nearly crushed that poor woman! It dawned on Tim that it would have actually been the second time the bag had crushed a woman. Oh no, thought Tim, what if this is actually some Tyler Durton[51] situation and I am the serial killer! Maybe I suppressed my crossdressing too well, and Brooke became her own person, someone who enjoys murdering people? It made too much sense. How else would someone have found every single one of his crossdressing graves? Why else was he out in the middle of the night disposing of evidence? Why else would the killer be a crossdresser? Wait a minute, wasn't he being chased by an axe-wielding maniac who was moments away from butchering him alive? He quickly turned around, expecting an axe in the face, but his pursuer was gone. Had he imagined her? The fear seemed so real. But how could she have not caught him? Even at full speed, he was barely moving.

Whatever the hell had just happened, he needed to get out of here before he was accused of attempted murder. As he once again attempted, and failed, to move quickly, he remembered the various promises about self-improvement he made on the condition of his continued existence. As he had, in fact, survived, it appeared he would have to go through with it and admit his crossdressing to his friends and family. Tim thought about this and, while he had invoked the name of supernatural

---

[51] Sorry for the spoilers, but I've already made several Fight Club jokes before this, so you should have seen this coming.

beings or deities or whatever, really he had made this promise to himself. And the great thing about promises to yourself is the only person you will disappoint by breaking them is you. Tim decided he could forgive himself. That worked out pretty well, he thought as his thighs rapidly shifted back and forth in the direction of his car.

It was a good night for this, thought Bart. Just the right amount of dark and gritty, like *The Dark Knight*. He would have settled for one of the Burton era films, which were plenty dark, but felt they didn't have enough grittiness. He wanted a night that was as far from *Batman and Robin* or *Superman vs Batman* as possible. Bart would have once dismissed having that much knowledge about a superhero as weak, nerdy and unmasculine. But now, thanks to Marvel, superheroes were all the rage, and society had adapted its definition of acceptably masculine behaviour to include them. It was strange how the only forces that could cause rapid changes in societal gender stereotypes were megacorporations.

To feel extra Batman-like, Bart would have preferred to be perched on a rooftop overlooking the street. However, he felt that was a bad idea as he wasn't confident in his new heels. His old favourites had been destroyed in that unfortunate incident with the corpse, and it was always a struggle to find heels that he could squeeze on the giant lumps of muscle attached to his ankles. These ones were a bit on the tight side, so he was in a fair amount of pain.

At this point, the reader is probably wondering why someone emulating Batman is dressed as a woman. Firstly, it's sexist to suggest Batman had to be played by a man. Secondly, Bart reasoned that Batman dressed as a Bat in order to invoke fear in his enemies. Right now, everyone was pretty afraid of crossdressers, so dressing up like this was the most Batman thing he could do. It wasn't because he liked it. It definitely wasn't because spending hours browsing for the perfect heels online was one of his favourite things. And it most certainly wasn't because of any nagging wish that he'd been born female. No, this was a necessity.

His ensemble was slightly ruined by the large fire axe he was carrying, although he had painted his nails red in a last-minute attempt to match it. Bart was a fireman, the manliest profession he could think of when he graduated high school, so he had easy access to some impressive axes. Unfortunately, they didn't have purse-sized axes in the firehouse and anyway, the idea of taking anything smaller than the largest axe he could was too unmanly for Bart to contemplate. Not to mention, he was going toe to toe with a potential serial killer and didn't want to go into that confrontation with some sad baby axe. So he patrolled down the street at two in the morning, axe in hand while his feet screamed in pain. Several hours of this had so far turned up nothing. They never showed this part in the movies, thought Bart, where Batman watches for several hours hoping for a mugging to happen so he can swoop in all heroically. He probably has some good games built into the suit, he must have a pretty damn good collection on Pokemon Go by now.

As he followed yet another line of thought concerning Batman, he almost didn't notice the woman walk out of an alleyway down the street. The woman turned and looked at him. At this point, Bart noticed the large duffle bag she was carrying. It looked almost identical to one he had launched out of his firepit the previous week, except this one had scorch marks on it. He took a few more painful steps forward, thinking how strange it was they had a similar bag, before putting two and two together. It was the same bag! How the hell did she get it? Then he remembered. It was a woman on the phone who threatened him that night and here, again, a woman. The pieces were falling into place. There really was a conspiracy to frame him for murdering that asshole! Well, he had them now. He smiled, gripped his axe and moved forward.

The woman looked panicked as Bart moved forward, and she attempted to flee. Normally Bart's impressive leg muscles would have made this chase something cheetahs watch in awe, wondering what they've been doing wrong all these years with the gazelles. But Bart's feet[52] were in dire straits. He could take off the heels, but he'd spent a good ten minutes getting his feet into them in the first place. He didn't like his chances of reversing the process. At this point, he'd be glad if they hadn't permanently fused into his skin. There was no time to worry about it as the murderer was getting away, albeit very slowly. It seemed they were also not dressed for pursuit. For a brief second, he admired their heels and felt sympathy for their feet before remembering they were his one chance at fixing all this and so resumed the chase. Bart gained a few inches on his target, but his right foot started buckling and appeared to be bleeding. Damn, he thought as the target regained those few hard-won inches.[53] He tried sliding his heel off with the blunt side of his axe, but that did nothing but smear blood all over the axe. Bart thought on his feet, although

---

[52] A lot of this chapter is talking about feet, so I wanted to make a play on words with "footnote", but I've got nothing.

[53] Technically, crossdressing is different from drag, and this is a chase, not a race. So RuPaul can't say I stole his idea. Then again, RuPaul's Drag Chase would be a pretty good name for a dating show spin-off of Drag Race. Fun fact: Googling "RuPaul's Drag Chase" to see if it already exists brings up nothing but articles about one of the Drag Race judges being arrested at a Chase Bank. This footnote has been a bit of a journey.

he didn't want to add too many thoughts to the pressure on them, and repurposed his fire axe as a walking stick.

With the weight off one of his feet, he started gaining again. Inch by inch, Bart got closer. His rage at this whole emasculating situation he had been put through the past week or so kept his focus off the mind-splitting pain that coursed through him with each step. All he needed to do was catch this woman, or man, or whoever the fuck they were, beat the shit out of her and drag her to the police, and all of this would be over. No more crossdressing, no more accidentally murdering anyone, no more staying up late hunting fugitives. He could go back to his normal life with Rosalind and live happily ever after, having dealt with the whole gender problem. Bart would show everyone how a good beatdown solves most of life's problems. As he relished the thought of his fist making contact with his enemy's face, and drew ever nearer to said enemy, his heel chose this moment to give way. He fell forward on the street and the mental dam holding back the mind-shattering pain coming from his foot collapsed. He rolled back and forth on the ground as a long series of swear words came out of him.

Stop it, he told himself. This isn't very Batman-like! Although it was normal for Batman to be bested by the villain before redeeming himself later in the movie. Like when Batman's back was broken by Bane. This was Bart's dark cave to crawl out of. He pulled himself up onto his knees in time to see the bastard throw the bag into the river. That thing was so polluted it would dissolve before he got down there. He'd lost his chance to prove the conspiracy around these murders. Remembering that the person he was watching might, in fact, be a murderer, Bart decided it would be best they didn't notice he had been critically disabled. They could take the opportunity for a bit of murdering, so he disappeared into the shadows of an alleyway. He imagined it as being like Batman dramatically whipping his cape around and disappearing into the shadows, but in reality, it was Bart crawling on fours into the alley, desperately trying to keep his skirt over his butt.

He watched the suspect flee the bridge. Next time, he thought as his anger simmered, next time he'd have proper shoes, and they wouldn't stand a chance. The real crime here was that his amazing manly calf muscles had been restrained from unleashing their overwhelming power. "See you soon," he said quietly as the probable murderer disappeared from view.

CHAPTER 5

Driving is good, thought Tim. You have to focus on the road. There's no time to think or worry or stress. A nice sturdy steering wheel to grip so your hands don't shake. Momentum to use if the need for self-defence arises. Glass and metal putting up a barrier between you and the rest of the world. And, of course, the possibility of escaping and driving off into the sunset if things get really bad.

The time for that may be fast approaching.

In the seat next to him was Mills, who had the case file sprawled out on her lap, peering on a surveillance photo of Tim leaving the station with the bag. "Smarmy motherfucker," she said. Tim tried to ignore her and focus on the road, but she continued. "Coming into to my station and stealing my evidence, making me look like a fucking idiot."

"I'm sure they weren't trying to do that," suggested Tim. "If anything, they're panicking because we're getting close."

"Panicking! Ha!" Mills let out a sarcastic laugh. "Then why lead us right to another stash of clothes? And the weird machine we pulled out of the river? No, they knew what they were fucking doing."

Tim didn't have a good answer for that. A CCTV camera had snagged a photo of him dumping the bag over the bridge and so the police had, of course, dragged the river. The first strange thing was they didn't find the bag. Tim figured it would still be sitting on the riverbank where he left it, but it had vanished. Did the person he almost murdered take it with them? Or is there a homeless person on the street somewhere in his clothes right now? That was worrying enough, but then the divers found another entire stash of semi dissolved women's clothing at the bottom of the river. This made him much more worried about his theory from the other night. Had Brooke been operating by herself and dumping clothes in the river? How long had this been going on? Was he more Brooke than Tim now? Was he losing his mind? He hadn't been able to sleep the past few nights, wondering if that's when she took over. The rings under his eyes had darkened a few shades, and he had lost several kilograms, even with a significant amount of stress eating. Actually, he didn't mind the weight loss. It would make it easier to fit some of the tighter dresses he had been eyeing off. Tim winced as he realised he was letting his mind wander to crossdressing again. Was Brooke trying to take over while he was still awake?

At the same time, the whole Brooke theory didn't make much sense. Why kill someone and use their body to lead the police to his stash of clothes? Why use his bag to crush another person? How would him being in prison help Brooke? Surely he would have noticed if his legs had suddenly been shaved overnight? It was beginning to seem unlikely. Tim wasn't sure what was more stressful: having a split personality with a mind of their own causing chaos or having no idea what was causing the chaos.

The Brooke theory certainly didn't explain the strange device in the back seat of the car, another thing the divers had pulled from the river. "What do you think it is?" Tim asked Mills, thinking maybe it would stop her from staring at the photo of him.

"If I knew that we wouldn't be driving out here," she said, the attempt failing to divert her attention from the photo for even a second. A few moments later, they came over a rise, and the giant DätaCorp campus appeared before them. It was a massive complex of ultramodern glass and steel buildings, with the headquarters in the shape of a large glass Klein bottle.[54] Toruses had been all the rage in IT headquarters since Apple had done it but DätaCorp was one step ahead of the topological game and had gone to the Klein bottle. The massive steel and glass structure almost blinded Tim as they drove towards it. Its highly reflective nature was responsible for three plane crashes per month on average. Thanks to DätaCorp's AI-powered legal division, it was cheaper to settle the lawsuits than to redesign the building.

A short drive later, they pulled up to the security gate at the entrance to the campus. Both of them flashed their badges to the guard as he walked over to the car. Mills didn't look up from her case files. "Ah," said the guard, "you must be here about the bag."

Mills diverted her attention from the photo to the guard. "What bag?"

Tim knew what bag. He clenched the steering wheel harder. The guard gave them directions and they soon arrived at a strange scene. An exclusion zone had been set up around a familiar looking bag. Near the centre, a small drone on six wheels and some small arms made its way towards the bag. In one of its hands was something Tim couldn't quite make out.

---

[54] I could try and explain what a Klien bottle is, but honestly, it'll just be faster if you Google it.

"It turned up this morning," explained the DätaCorp technician supervising the operation. "Figured it was another bomb."

"Another bomb?" asked Tim. "This has happened before?"

"Oh yeah, all the time. You don't eat into a significant share of the weapons market without making enemies with access to explosives."

The small drone inched closer and repositioned its arm. "It's getting ready to place the charge so we can blow it," explained the technician.

"Blow it!" yelled Mills. "That's my fucking evidence. You can't blow it!"

"You sure? I mean, how often do you get to see a robot blow something up! It's pretty cool."

"I don't care. It's mine!"

Tim saw an opportunity, "You know the murderer has been unpredictable up to this point. Maybe it is a bomb!"

"I don't think that's their MO."

"Well, they don't really have much of a consistent strategy. It might be the safe thing to do." Mills stared down Tim. "Plus, you know, like the guy said, how often do we get to blow shit up?"

Mills let out a breath of annoyance. "If they want to blow me up, they can fucking try," and with that, she walked past the drone and grabbed the bag. Mills was so angry that even if there had been a bomb in the bag, she would have diffused it with pure force of will. The drone looked confused. Without the bag, its life lacked purpose. Technicians would have to patch this existential crisis out of its firmware later.

"Aww," said the DätaCorp technician. "Would have been fun."

"Right, fuck you, we need you to have a look at this device."

Mills grabbed the guy and dragged him down to their car with Tim in tow. She threw open the door. "What the fuck is it?" she asked the man.

The technician was annoyed. No one would dare treat him this way once he had a personal drone army. He looked over the device in the backseat. "That's one of our phallometers, probably the one that got stolen the other week."

"Phallowhat?" asked Tim, but Mills cut in.

"Why didn't you report it?"

"Well," said the technician, summoning all his condescension, "we're generally better at finding things than the police."

"Well, I can make sure no one ever finds you," said Mills in a tone that made Tim and the technician believe her. "I'll ask again. What the fuck is it?"

The man rolled his eyes. "It's a device for measuring blood flow to the penis. To dumb it down, it's a magic box that tells you how aroused someone is. We use it for security clearances for recruitment, but also our advertising division gets some use out of it too."

Mills calmed down. "Why the hell would a murderer be interested in that?"

"Dunno," said the technician.

Mills looked silently in thought at the device for a few moments. "You know," she said to Tim, "we know the killer is getting some sort of sexual thrill from all this since they left all those condoms around the second victim. This device might be exactly what we need."

"What do you mean?"

"We can use it to screen people. Finding all the people who get a thrill from dressing up all girly would at least give us a list of suspects."

Tim didn't like where this was going. "What about civil liberties? We can't force everyone into some weird polygraph-style interrogation."

The DätaCorp technician wasn't sure if he was still needed or not but was too afraid of Mills to leave, so he stood around awkwardly and wondered what the hell this civil liberties thing was.

"No one would be forced," said Mills. "But if they refused, they'd end up on the list of suspects."

"This is going too far, Mills," said Tim.

Mills walked right up to him. "They took it too far." She prodded his chest. "They came into my station and messed with my shit. They declared war." She turned and pointed at the technician, "How much for one of these?"

"I'm sure we can come up with something in your price range," he smiled.

Mills nodded. "And you guys build surveillance tech, right?"

"We sure do. For a modest price, I'm sure we could set you up with some surveillance drones. Their AI can be programmed to search for targets."

Mills smirked. "So you could make them search for, say, men dressed as women."

"I'm sure the AI boys could come up with a model for that."

"Mills," interjected Tim. "You can't screen the entire neighbourhood while an army of drones patrols it! This isn't a police state!"

"It is now," said Mills. "First things first. The fact that they got into our station makes me suspicious. I think we need to make sure we're clean, so we test the station before starting with the wider community."

"Mills, this is crazy! I think you've gone a little bit off the rails."

Mills gave him a look that people only usually encountered when they were on the receiving end of a truncheon., "You just volunteered to be the first one we test!"

"What!"

"Stay here and watch the bag while I go sort all this out. Who do I see about buying this stuff?" she asked the technician.

"If you follow me this way, I can take you to our sales team," he said smugly as he and Mills walked off towards one of the glass and steel blocks.

Fuck fuck fuck, thought Tim, he was completely fucked. Once Mills was out of sight, he started his physical panicking. He paced back and forth, occasionally kicking the bag, letting out the odd "fuck", completely at a loss as to what to do. He really needed a beer, but that seemed a long shot. Could he pass this phallometer thing? Did he crossdress for some weird kink? He didn't feel like that, but the thrill of it gave him some sort of a reaction down there sometimes. Why did he crossdress? He'd never really thought about why he did it. It was just something he felt an urge to do from time to time. Was he in it for the thrills or was it something deeper? Was it some unchangeable part of himself, some part of his identity?

Tim shook his head. He shouldn't be wasting time thinking about this. What was he on about anyway? He wasn't a crossdresser! He hadn't worn women's clothing for at least – he checked his watch – 35 hours now, and that had definitely been the last time. He'd said that before, but he hadn't predicted the strange series of events that would involve him stealing from his own police station. He wasn't a crossdresser. It was like a mouth burn or a pimple. The more you poked it, the longer it took to heal. He always had been a poker. He just needed willpower. But would willpower be enough to stop any reaction to the phallometer? He wasn't confident. He needed a backup plan.

The room was a sea of diversity. You had trans men and trans women, intersex people. Various types of non-binary genders, including trinary, quaternary and even one sexagesimal. There were several viscosities of gender fluidity, ranging from treacle to liquid helium levels. There was a mass of genderqueerness including bigenders, agenders, neutrois, demiguys, demigirls, pangenders, polygenders and more. Not to mention the other queerness of the rooms from homosexuals, bisexuals, trisexuals, asexuals, bsexuals, pansexuals, potsexualsm, polysexuals, pretty much any Latin sounding prefix together with sexual. All of them displaying their identity with complete pride and no fear. Amongst all this diversity and pride was one man feeling very uncomfortable about it all. Stan was sitting next to Julia and Rosalind, who had for some reason insisted on coming with him. Julia looked quite proud of the scene in front of her, but Rosalind looked even more uncomfortable than Stan felt, if that was possible. Best he could figure was that Julia was still trying to convince Rosalind to stop hanging around with the Coalition for Calmdressing. Stan was fairly sympathetic to the group. They shared his goal of reducing the number of crossdressers in town. However, their methods were much more archaic and brutal than what he'd planned, and his plans were what forced him to be here.

Though he hated to admit it, Stan knew he couldn't do everything with theory alone. He needed experimental data to confirm his work. If the unlikely happened and it turned out his theoretical framework was wrong, then any attempt at a treatment plan he developed from his theory could, in the worst case, exacerbate his symptoms. The last thing he needed was an incorrect assumption about the cardinality of a normal subgroup to cause him to end up going from part-time crossdresser to full transgender. He needed trial groups, placebo groups, all that stuff, before he dared test it on himself. Stan didn't want to be in the middle of this throng of diversity, but he was in search of test subjects, and this was the easiest way to find other people who shared his affliction.

He wasn't as ready as he would like to be, but his plans had been accelerated by events beyond his control. Somehow the police had decided dredging the river was a good idea, and they had found what was left of his nights as Loreta and probably the phallometer. The chance of them finding anything forensically tying him to any of it was slim, but Stan was paranoid. He planned his life around worst-case scenarios to such a degree that he avoided being in photographs in case he was somehow responsible for a future apocalypse and people would be sent back in time to kill him. If someone traced him back to that bag, he needed to be able to say under whatever interrogation he was subjected to that he was definitely not a crossdresser, which would be a lot easier if he was not actually a crossdresser.

On top of that, he still had the DätaCorp conspiracy to deal with. At first, he was at a loss at what to do with the bag they had hurled at him in their clever intimidation attempt. But then he realised there was only one proportional response to intimidation, showing them you don't give a shit. So, late last night, he'd snuck into DätaCorp again, and dumped the bag right on their doorstep. As if to say: "Here's your bag.

I knew it was you the whole time, assholes. You can't scare me!" Even if only one of those statements were true. Now he thought about it, calling out a mega-corporation that produces weapons and is currently being investigated by multiple war crimes tribunals might have been a bad idea. But Stan's train of thought was interrupted as someone got up from the crowd.

"Hi everyone," said a person of unidentified gender with short purple hair and enough piercings that Stan could feel them in his face. "I'm the Pax Gardens Pride Network's event coordinator, Amy Stake[55] and my pronouns are they, them. Welcome to today's catch-up session. I hope the speech therapist we had talk last week was helpful for those of you who have voice dysphoria and are looking for options to try and deal with that. Today we have another speaker, an academic who is going to give a talk about some research they have been doing into gender diversity." The presenter gestured at Stan, who got up and started wheeling a whiteboard he had brought with him to the front of the room.

"Thanks for having me," said Stan, pulling the cap off a whiteboard marker. "I'm Stan, and I'm going to talk you through the theoretical structure of gender I've come up with. Now—"

"Umm, sorry to interrupt," Amy interjected from the front row, "But usually, we give our pronouns when we introduce ourselves."

"Pronouns?"

"Yes, you know, how do you refer to yourself: He, she, they, maybe one of the more modern ones like ze?"

---

[55] While deciding their name during their transition, they asked their father what they would have called them if they had been born female. Their father replied: "The same thing I call you now: a mistake."

Stan thought about this for a second before replying with "Doctor."

"Umm, I don't think you quite understand—"

"I didn't spend three years on that PhD to be called something as generic as they," he said with extra disdain heaped on the word they.

At this point Amy thought that maybe this wasn't a good idea, but they were a very accepting person and didn't want to stop Stan from expressing dr's gender in a way that dr felt comfortable.

"Okay, now." Stan started furious scribbling on the whiteboard. "If we assume gender to be a field with permittivity of this constant and sexuality as a field with permeability of this, then we can apply Maxwell's equations, and we soon see—"

Suddenly Stan was cut off by an outburst in the audience. "What is wrong with all you people!" cried out Rosalind as she abruptly stood up. "You're not meant to be like this!"

"Rosalind! Sit down!" said Julia, tugging on Rosalind's dress.

Rosalind ignored her and kept talking. "Why don't you want to be normal? Live like a normal man or woman, have a normal hair colour and a more appropriate number of piercings. You're meant to want to have that happily ever after, married with a baby and a dog living in a nice house in the suburbs, having dinner parties with your neighbours who also have a baby and a dog and share photos of each other's baby and dog. You people are ruining it for everyone. The fewer people who want that ending, the harder it is for us good normal people to find it! It's selfish, really! And even if you're lucky enough to find a partner these days, your neighbours are probably going to be some strange non-binary couple who believe gender is an illusion, have no baby and, even worse, probably own a cat."

"What's wrong with cats?" said Julia, a closeted crazy cat lady.[56]

"Horrible for your skin, all that clawing," said Rosalind, wincing at the very thought of anything happening to the layer of cells she had spent so much time cultivating. "And dogs are better at posing for Instagram photos."

At this point, the crowd started booing and jeering Rosalind, yelling at her to get lost. "No Disney movie ever ended with a non-binary person finding happiness. It's all princesses finding true love with a handsome prince. That's how you should be finding happiness."

"Technically, most of them end in fantasy worlds with castles and talking animals, not a family and a house on a quarter acre," added Julia.

"I don't know why you dragged me here," Rosalind said before she finally gave in to the pressure from the crowd and fled the hall, with Julia running after her.

"Sorry about that," said Amy. "We get these crazy right-wing nutjobs in here sometimes. It's gotten worse since those calmdressers started their little hate group."

"Right," said Stan. "Well, back to what I was saying about Maxwell's equations." Stan resumed writing on the whiteboards. He'd run out of room on his first board and started further scribbles on another as the audience watched

---

[56] Julia may have actually been infected with toxoplasmosis, a parasite normally found in mice whose reproductive cycles require a cat's stomach. Infected mice become attracted to cats and are usually eaten as a result. Some people have speculated that humans infected with this parasite might explain why some people become obsessed with cats. It would also explain why, after a particular rave and under the influence of some powerful hallucinogens, Julia attempted several times to force-feed herself to her cat.

on with no idea what this strange man was talking about or why he was there at all.

⁓

If there was one thing Joe really hated in this world, it was man buns. He knew he wasn't in a position to judge, being a crossdresser and all, but he still really hated hipsters and their stupid man buns. What a waste of hair. Think of all the cute feminine styles you could pull off with that length. A nice bob, an elegant ponytail with a layered fringe, some gorgeous blonde highlights. God how he wished he could grow his hair out and have that be his life, changing hairstyles every month or two. He thought this as he stared at one of the DätaCorp executives sitting across the table from him. He had a rather prominent man bun together with an expertly sculpted beard. The beard raised Joe's opinion slightly. Now beards were something Joe could get behind. It was really the only fashionable thing men had over women.[57] He enjoyed styling his in a variety of different ways, from the hipster goatee the executive was displaying, though Joe thought he could do better, to ironic 19th-century style moustaches, to the art of creating exactly the right amount of stubble to give you the sexy unshaved look. That one was always the hardest. It took hours of effort in front of a mirror micromanaging his follicles to get the perfect unmanaged carefree look, but it was worth it.

In a perfect world, Joe would probably be a bearded woman. He had actually tried to get Stan to come up with a cream or gel or something that would allow women to grow temporary beards. It would be a marketing coup. Imagine a

---

[57] Unless you count most of the power and money in society as fashionable which, of course, Joe did.

world where women had facial hair to style! Think of all the crazy ideas they would come up with that would cost a fortune in conditioners and styling gels to create. But Stan told him such a thing wouldn't be possible without invasive surgery or the advent of nanotechnology, so he had to shelve that idea. Joe didn't view that as his failure though. It was really god's. What kind of deity has eternity and all the knowledge of the universe at his disposal and only comes up with two models for their main product line? Why not have a beard as a standard extra for the female model? Where's the sports model? Or a deluxe model that throws in the best features of the others with some extra leg room? Maybe a convertible model so you can enjoy all the privileges of being a man during the week, then pop the top and have some breasts for the weekend? Of course, anyone who had read the bible knew god had marketing problems. Come to that, anyone who had ever met a missionary,[58] or who had heard of the Catholic church.

Joe realised he was letting his mind wander and attempted to refocus on the task at hand. As well as the manbunned individual, there was a second executive across the table from him. This person was clearly more tech than executive and had been in the company at the right time to jump the ranks when its market value exploded. He wore a t-shirt that displayed a joke about an esoteric programming language only 17 people on the planet had ever used, as well as a pair of jeans so expensive that

---

[58] In 2018 the uncontacted Sentinelese Islanders killed a missionary who visited their island in an attempt to convert them. Most people think this is because of a general fear of outsiders, but this is only half true. Due to the large amount of plastic pollution that washed up on the island, the islanders had a fair idea of what marketing was and had, rightly so, decided it was something they didn't want in their society. The moment that young man tried to sell them anything, he was doomed. If he had approached silently and respectfully, they probably would have just roughed him up a bit.

their fake tears and wear marks perfectly made them look like an overworn $30 pair of jeans from Kmart.

Joe would need all his charisma working flawlessly to convince these DätaCorp executives to destroy whatever was left on the email account Claire had set up. So he had taken out all the stops, taken the two DätaCorp suits he had the best relationship with to the swankiest bar in town. He had prepped all his best jokes, spent hours practising them in the mirror. This was his one chance. He couldn't blow it. It was difficult for Joe to win over men. Ideally, he would have seduced some of DätaCorp's female executives to get what he needed. But unfortunately, he had already slept with several of them to secure an increased fee for his consulting firm's contract with the mega-corporation, and retreading that ground was too dangerous.

Joe's knowledge of how to manipulate men was limited to the Dregs, and that was child's play. You buy Tim a drink, tell Stan how smart he is, and compliment Bart on his enormous muscles. Joe mentally shrugged his shoulders. It wasn't like he had a better plan.

"So, can I get you guys a drink?" he asked.

The two executives picked up a drinks menu from the table and gave it a quick peruse, "Hmm, we'll take two of the pure dark ales."

"Pure dark?"

"According to the menu: It's brewed in a vault in Greenland several kilometres underground. The vault is completely electromagnetically sealed, sterile, soundproofed, and hermetically sealed. The brewing process is entirely automated, so it can be completely free of outside influence. The bottles are also perfectly sealed against the outside world. The first time this beer will ever experience any part of our universe is the moment it touches your tongue, letting you sample something that has come from the void."

"Sounds good," said Joe and grabbed a passing waiter to ask for a round of three. Three matte black bottles of ale were promptly delivered to their table. "Nice bottle art," said Joe as they cracked them open and had a taste. "Huh, you can really taste the abyss. Great choice Matt, impressive."

The manbunned individual, now identified as Matt, eyed him suspiciously and gave him a tentative "thank you."

"I mean, I would have probably just gone for a shitty pale ale." They all took another sip and felt something absorbing part of their souls. "Have you guys been working out? You look ripped."

"Okay, that's enough," said Matt, putting his bottle down. "We're not going to sleep with you, Joe."

"What?"

"I mean, it's pretty obvious what you're doing. Taking us to this bar, our usual place to trawl for chicks, trying to get us drunk, giving us those lame compliments. Clearly, you want some sort of horrible man sandwich to happen, and we're not into that."

"No, we are not," said the other executive.

"What? No, I'm not trying to sleep with you!" The thought of the man bun even being in the same postcode when he was sleeping with someone was enough to make him completely flaccid.

"Well, you clearly want something."

Joe sighed. "Alright, fine, I'll level with you. Someone is trying to blackmail me. Unfortunately, they passed away, but they've left a dead man's switch on a DätaCorp controlled email account. I'm asking for a favour: can you switch it off?"

The two executives looked at each other, then back to Joe. "That's very interesting, Joe," said Matt, taking another sip of his beer. "You see, when someone dies, everything in their account becomes property of DätaCorp."

"Wait, what? Really? You don't just wipe it."

The Tech Exec laughed. "Why would we throw away precious data? Most people don't realise it's what we do because it's on page 23,834 of our user agreement. Most people's computers will run out of memory and crash trying to load that far into the document."

"Okay, great, so you guys own it. Should be easy to turn it off then."

"Well, you see, here's the thing," said Matt. "What this effectively means is this person's blackmail material is now DätaCorp's blackmail material. We now own that contract, so you'll need to pay us the money."

"What!"

The Tech Exec had been fiddling on his phone while Matt had been explaining the situation and now chimed in "According to our AI investment analysis, your estimated blackmailable value is fifty thousand dollars."

Joe looked at both of them for a few seconds, stunned. "You can't be serious. We're friends!"

"Yes, but unfortunately, this is the company policy in these sorts of situations. We can't bend on it."

"Please, Matt," begged Joe. "We go way back. I even got your son a presale pair of swim jeans, for god's sake."

"Yes, well, he almost drowned in those."

"Did he read the label?[59] You're not meant to actually try swimming in them. Just stand in waist-deep water and look cool."

---

[59] The label on a pair of Swim Jeans reads as follows: Do not dry clean, machine wash, press, iron, fold, hang, swim in or wear in the vicinity of an open flame.

Matt sighed, "Look, we could take the money in the form of a reduced price for your firm's contract with DätaCorp."

"Are you insane!" said Joe. "My management will never go for that."

"Well then, you'd better find the money some other way," said Matt as he got up. "Good luck."

"I suggest speculative DataCoin[60] trading," said the Tech Exec following Matt's lead in leaving the table. "Made me a fortune."

Once again, Joe found himself at a table alone and depressed after being blackmailed. There was a certain feeling of deja vu to it. Worst of all, he'd been screwed over by the fine print. That was his thing! He was meant to be the one doing that to clients, charging exorbitant exit fees when they realise a consulting contract is completely worthless. It was humiliating. No way was he going to give them the money, that's for sure. However, they'd left him with limited options. It would require some sort of counter-blackmail scheme, hopefully, better than the last one. He took another sip of his ale, felt the cold emptiness of the void and started thinking.

∽

Stan wiped the sweat from his forehead as he finished the final line on the whiteboard. "So, as you can see here, we've reduced the problem to several composite problems which we can solve so long as we can prove the Reimann hypothesis, that Zermelo–Fraenkel set theory is logically consistent and unify general relativity with quantum mechanics." He tapped his pen on one equation on the board. "I think I'm close

---

[60] DataCoin was DätaCorp's blockchain cryptocurrency. The market price of one DataCoin is so volatile that most computers have switched to using it as their source of entropy for random number generation.

on the Reimann hypothesis." He turned to the audience. "Questions?"

The audience responded with a look that was a mixture of stunned and confused. After several seconds of silence, a hand raised. "You keep referring to 'the problem'. What exactly are you trying to solve?"

"Oh, sorry, I thought that was obvious: the gender problem."

The crowd let out a mixture of confused and angry murmuring. "What gender problem?"

"Well, you know, the issue that you—" Stan almost said we but fortunately caught himself "—all are suffering from. If we can find a way to fix that, then maybe we can stop this murderer going around town."

"Ah shit," said a transman in the crowd, "This is some pray the gay away bullshit isn't it?"

A series of boos and jeers were hurled from the crowd at Stan. That didn't bother him, but the idea of any of his work being compared to something as ridiculous as praying was hugely insulting.

"I'm so sorry, everyone," said Amy. "I didn't realise what this speaker's true agenda was. Obviously this talk is over."

"No, let the bigot speak. Let's see if he can convince us," said the unidentified transman, who was met with laughter and applause.

"Umm, okay if that's what everyone wants. Just let me point out that the Pax Gardens Pride Network doesn't support, uhh, dr's viewpoints."

"Maybe it would help if I illustrated the problem a bit better," said Stan, and he quickly drew up a series of bar graphs. "If you look at average earnings, healthcare outcomes and general happiness levels, you can see that people such as yourselves are far worse off than…" Stan was going to say normal people but didn't want to be yelled at again. "…people who aren't you."

"Yeah, that's called systemic discrimination," shouted someone from the audience and was met by another chorus of agreement.

"I'm not saying it's your fault." Stan was trying his very best to keep his arrogance at bay. He really needed to win them over. "But this is cold hard data showing you that being closer to the norm is better."

"You're right about that being a problem, but the solution isn't to try and 'fix' us," said a non-binary individual in the audience. "It's to fix society!" This time there was applause.

"Well, I mean, that is a solution, but from an engineering point of view, it's not optimal. If we're aiming for maximum societal happiness with the minimum effort, it's far more efficient to try and change one per cent of society than to try and change the other ninety-nine per cent."[61]

The crowd started booing him again, and Stan started to lose what little friendliness he had been trying to inject into his demeanour. "I just don't understand why you'd be against being normal," he said to the crowd.

"We are normal!"

"Yeah!" yelled the crowd.

"Well, statistically speaking, you're not." Stan drew a quick normal distribution on one of the whiteboards and put a small dot far off to one side, "This dot is you. You're at least several sigmas out of the average. If this were CERN, we'd be calling you a new particle by now."

---

[61] Of course, ninety-nine per cent of the world's wealth is held by one per cent of people. So, by Stan's logic, you think you could solve a lot of things by, say, taxing that one per cent. But for some reason no one ever seems to try this.

There were only a few people in the crowd with enough knowledge of particle physics to get the joke, and they had too much disdain for Stan to acknowledge it with a laugh.

"Don't you get it? If you could be normal, you wouldn't have to obsess over this anymore. No more sleepless nights wondering what to do. You could just go and hang out with your friends, have fun like old times, not have to worry about what they would think. You could just..." Stan paused and added softly "...be."

"What kind of shit friends wouldn't accept us?" This was met by a communal "Yeah!" from the crowd.

"Well, you know," said Stan, "Not everyone is accepting. You don't want to have to pick and choose friends."

"Bullshit. We're not the problem. It's those people. We've all met them, the little fratriarchal guy groups who talk about women like they're conquests, drink themselves stupid and treat the tiny sign of femininity in each other as something to be derided and ridiculed. Groups of men who haven't grown or changed in any meaningful way since primary school but still think they're the best because they conform to some sort of ridiculous heteronormative ideal. It's pathetic. Who'd want them as friends?"

At this point, Stan was fuming. You can insult him, question the quality of his maths, reject his excellent reasoning and, worst of all, ignore his hilarious particle-based jokes. But no one insults the Dregs.

"You know what? Fuck all of you! You want to be a bunch of freaks, fine. I'm out of here." Stan furiously pulled on his whiteboard but in the process of explaining his masterpiece, they had all gotten jammed into each other. He tugged a few times in awkward fury before giving up. "I'll come back later for these!" he yelled and stormed out.

"Good luck with whatever it is you're repressing!" someone from the crowd yelled out.

"Fuck you!" Stan yelled back as he walked out the door.

Those people don't know what they're on about, thought Stan. They can't accept help when it's given to them on a silver platter. He sighed as he walked towards his car. Without them, he didn't have a large enough sample to test his models against. He had no way of knowing the best way to cure himself. And now he was up against the police as well as DätaCorp. He didn't have time to try and find more test subjects. There was one option left. Stan didn't like it, but it was his only choice.

⌒∾

Dr Viola rocked back in her chair with a deep exhale as her last client for the day left her consulting room. That last patient had multiple personalities, each more of a jerk than the one before, and was exhausting. She really didn't want to write up her notes right now. Reluctantly, she opened her laptop but decided instead to procrastinate a little and checked the news. The headline was a story about the crossdressing serial killer stealing evidence from the police lookup and dumping it at the local DätaCorp offices. This had Dreg written all over it.[62] They were all obviously, in technical terms, quite mad. She gave herself a mental reminder to send that report about Tim to his superiors. But did any of them seem like they were capable of murder? Well, Stan did, but he didn't have the physical strength. At least one of the murders involved hurling heavy bags at people. Tim probably would be too tipsy to be coordinated enough to

---

[62] This was a common occurrence to anyone who passed out at a Dreg hosted party.

have done them. And Joe wouldn't do anything that could ruin his precious reputation, like murder. But she still felt a group of mentally unsound crossdressers coming onto her radar right when crossdressers were killing people was too much of a coincidence. The police needed to know. But they had all taken her into their confidence, and she didn't have definitive proof they were a threat to themselves or others. She groaned and rubbed her eyes as she failed to think of a good solution to all of this.

Suddenly, her door swung open, and a bulky man walked into her office. The floorboards creaking under the strain.

"I'm sorry, but my hours are over for the day. I can make you an appointment for another time if you wish," she said as she put her glasses back on and brought up her calendar on her laptop.

"That's not why I'm here," said Bart as he walked over to her desk and towered above her, "I need the names of all your patients who are crossdressers."

⌒

After his failed patrol the previous evening, Bart had rethought his strategy. Tracking down crossdressers while roaming the streets had been surprisingly successful. Catching them was trickier. While a lot of what Batman does is just patrolling the night, looking for mobsters to swoop down on, he is also the world's greatest detective. So Bart had wiped the dust off his brain and fired it up for the first time since his last high school exam, and it had worked surprisingly well. He reasoned that anyone who dresses as a woman and murders people probably has some issues, so there was a good chance they had seen a psychologist about it. All he had to do was go to the psychs around town and get a list of any crossdressing patients from them. Then it would be time to shut down his brain again and power up his fists.

"Well, I'm sorry," said Dr Viola, "but those records are confidential."

"I thought you might say that," said Bart, and he slammed a wad of cash down on the desk.

"Sorry, I took an oath," she said as looked down at the bulging bicep that had deposited the cash. Anger took over her face. "Oh for fuck's sake, you're a Dreg, aren't you?"

"Damn," muttered Bart, "Of course you would recognise me. We're just too damn notorious." It was just another way he was like Batman. His alter ego was too famous. That's why Batman wore a mask. Bart's disguise had been his crossdressing, now that was dangerous in broad daylight. He'd gone looking for masks, but the only ones in the stores were cheap plastic ones for five-year-olds. A cartoony cow face wasn't as intimidating as a bat.

Dr Viola rubbed her eyes in frustration and groaned. "Let me guess why you're here. You have a secret habit of dressing up as a woman." Bart's stoic exterior of manliness crumpled into fear. "And you're trying to find the crossdressing serial killer so that everything goes back to normal and people stop trying to uncover crossdressers and the other Dregs never learn your secret. Is that a good summary?"

Bart stood there with his mouth gaping open for a few seconds, "What— No— you don't know what you're talking about!" he eventually stammered, then shouted.

"Oh god, you're just so textbook. You scream masculine, don't you? You think if you act manly enough, the girly will just go away?"

"Shut up!" Once again, he slammed his hands down on her desk.

"And the anger is so predictable." A series of muscles in Bart's limbs started to contract and his fist tightened. Dr Fiola took the hint. "Look, let's just talk about this," she said in a much calmer tone. "You think that if you solve these murders, it will all just magically go away. Well it won't. You should deal with your feelings and tell the Dregs the truth." She could see Bart's muscles loosen as he thought about what she said. "You can talk to me. As a therapist I'm not allowed to tell anyone anything unless you're a threat to yourself or others."

Bart looked downwards for a few seconds, this thoughtfulness a rare facial expression for him, before looking up again. "You don't understand. I'm the best of the Dregs, their leader.[63] It would be devastating to them if they found out."

Dr Viola looked dubious at the suggestion Bart was the leader of the Dregs. "That's not how leadership works. You don't just do what everyone else expects of you. You lead them to better ways."

Bart laughed. "Yeah, running around in a skirt, much better way. Maybe just stick to dealing with crazy people and give me the names already so I can sort this all out."

"The Dregs don't see you as a leader. They fear you. That's what really controls the Dregs. If you told them the truth, you could remove all the fear and all of you could just be yourselves!"

"It's not fear. It's respect. I mean, look at me." He flexed various bulges of muscle in his forearm while Dr Viola rolled her eyes. "I'm an amazing specimen. They all wish they were

---

[63] The Dregs had actually once attempted to elect a leader, but it had resulted in a 4-way tie in the votes. The supreme Dreg court was also unable to resolve this as all four chief justices had come to different conclusions about the election result, leading to a Dregstitutional crisis that continues to this day.

the man I am. You think they'll respect me if they find out about all this?"

"Yes, absolutely."

Bart shook his head. "I'll take those names now."

Dr Viola took a deep breath and stared him down. "It's time you left my office."

There was a cold silence for a few seconds, then Bart's eyes fell on her laptop, "I need those names. It's the only way to clear my name." He reached for the laptop but Dr Viola pulled it away just in time, before springing out of her chair. He edged his way around the desk. She moved to keep the desk between them.

"They're not going to accuse you of murder for being a crossdresser. You should just leave."

"I can't."

Dr Viola looked confused, but then her eyes grew wide. "Oh my god, you killed those people."

Bart stopped moving for a second, "No, I didn't. Well one of them, sort of, but it wasn't my fault!"

Dr Viola grabbed her phone and started dialling.

"What are you doing?"

"I'm calling the police."

"What? But you said this was all confidential unless I was a threat to myself or others!"

"You killed someone!"

"Yes, but that's in the past. I was a threat, and I'm no longer a threat," he said as he began edging around the table again.

Dr Viola once again manoeuvred to keep the desk between them. "I'm feeling pretty threatened right now."

"I don't know why you would," he said as he yanked the phone cable out of the wall. "We're just talking," he said in a tone that he hoped would be as calm and non-threatening.

Unfortunately, Bart had little experience in being calm or non-threatening. His tone was basically unchanged. In reality, Bart would never hurt a woman. A lot of his views might be from a century or two ago and be very sexist, but he did view violence against women as abhorrent.

The phone line went dead, Dr Viola looked at her purse, which contained her mobile, but there was a large emotionally unstable man between her and it. Luckily for her, by now, she and Bart had done a 180 around the desk, and she started backing towards the door. "Bart, if it really was an accident, you should tell the police. I'm sure they would understand."

"Oh, it's not the police that are the problem. They're trying to set me up!"

"They?"

"I don't know who they are, but they somehow planted that bag and killed that woman. It's some anti-Dreg conspiracy!"

Bart glared at Dr Viola with a realisation. "You're part of it, aren't you? That's why you won't give me the names!"

"Jesus, would you listen to yourself?" Dr Viola was still a fair distance from the door. Making a break for it wouldn't work. "Screw it! I think this is reasonable grounds for breaking patient confidentiality. Bart, listen, there's something you need to know about your friends that will fix all of this. Your friends, they're al—" she was abruptly cut off when she slipped on a misplaced ornamental onion, fell backwards and snapped her neck, killing her instantly.

The office was deathly silent. All Bart could do was stare blankly at the situation in front of him, before sighing and saying, "God-fucking-damn it."

CHAPTER 6

If there were one word that the Dregs would use to describe Stan's apartment, sterile would be a top contender. Today it was even more sterile than usual. The smell of bleach permeated the whole apartment and every bit of furniture was covered with plastic sheeting. In the middle of the living room, Stan was setting up everything he needed. There was a table with bandages, some medical alcohol, a small microchip, a textbook, a laptop and a drill. Next to this was a chair set up with a strange rig holding a downwards-facing camera looking at the seat, with a stream of cables connecting it to the laptop. All his other plans having failed, he had no choice but to go back to the idea he had discussed with Dr Viola: deep brain stimulation. The fact that she was now dead, apparently murdered, drove his sense of urgency. Right now, there was most likely an entire team of forensic experts pouring over her patient records, not to mention the rumours about the police now having their own phallometer.

The microchip had been surprisingly easy to acquire. Since Elon Musk had put one in a pig's brain, an endless number of tech startups began selling brain implants ranging from the deep brain stimulation model Stan required, to full wifi brain interfaces and simple thought-powered garage door openers.

The challenging part was to get them to ship it before the company collapsed under the weight of lawsuits from brain-damaged customers.

With a serial killer on the loose, the rest of the supplies had been trickier to get hold of. DätaCorp could still be watching him so he didn't want to purchase online, but you can't just walk into Bunnings and ask which drill would have the best penetrating power against a human skull. He'd been forced to buy bones at a butcher shop so he could test different models when no one was watching. That had been mildly annoying but bulk buying bleach and plastic sheeting was worse. Bleach wasn't so bad. He went to multiple suppliers and bought small quantities. Most supermarkets sell it in small quantities, but not many places sell surgical-grade plastic sheeting. Of those that do, few accept cash, and they are a long way from each other. It took hours of driving to accumulate enough. Luckily, most stores accepted his germaphobia story.

Perhaps the hardest aspect to deal with had been his head, specifically his hair. He couldn't do open brain surgery on himself with his magnificent chestnut locks in the way. He would have to shave his head. It was the most feminine part of his entire body. During an evening as Loreta, everything else was fake: his padded bra, contoured makeup to make his face look more feminine, a girdle and hip padding to give him a better figure. But the hair was real, the one genuinely womanly part of him. He reasoned that once he had the chip in his head, he wouldn't feel these horrible feminine cravings anymore, and the state of his hair would have no bearing on his happiness. And in the end, if it came down to choosing between being accepted by the Dregs and his hair, there was no contest. Still, the act of cutting his hair had been the hardest part. A few tears rolled down his cheeks as reams of hair fell to the floor. But it was done now, he thought as he felt his now completely smooth head. No choice but to move forward.

Right, he thought. Everything was ready. He took a deep breath. All he had to do was get through this one horrible thing, and then he'd be normal. Normal. The word made him smile. He thought about how great it would be. He would fit right at the peak of a normal distribution, look down upon all the less-than-average people and feel superior. It would be fantastic. And finally, he would fit in completely with the Dregs. Once he got rid of this crossdressing compulsion, other normal things would follow. He would start enjoying sport, maybe actually grow a beard, try out this womanising thing Joe seemed to enjoy. Sure, there was a slight chance of brain damage, but the Dregs were more likely to accept him with minor brain damage than in a skirt. After all, they loved Bart as much as any other Dreg, despite him having suffered enough concussions that any doctor would probably diagnose him with brain damage.

Stan took a seat in the chair with the rig above it, the laptop now displaying a segment of his bald head. He looked at the table. There was a brain anatomy textbook open to a top-down view of the brain as well as some MRI images he had gotten after that particularly drunken weekend of manliness which eventually involved a 'how many beans can you fit up your nose' contest. He would have preferred some functional MRIs to narrow down the location of where the chip should go, but he thought he had enough information to get at least close to the right place. He made a few marks on his skull with a texta and started positioning the drill in the rig.

He took a few deep breaths. It'll be over soon, he told himself. All you've got to do is drill through the skull, put the chip in, then bandage up the wound. It'll take two minutes tops. It'll be fine. He took another few deep breaths, started the drill up and slowly lowered the rigging towards his head. He could hear the whirring getting louder and his bald head felt a slight breeze from the spinning tip's approach.

At this point, it's worth mentioning the fatal flaw in Stan's plan. Apart from the potentially literal fatal aspects. Unfortunately, Stan was extremely squeamish and needle phobic. He couldn't take a simple injection without passing out. He would probably have been an anti-vaxxer if it weren't for the fact his IQ was above seven.

The drill touched the top of his scalp, and he instantly passed out in his rig. Fortunately, Stan was paranoid and had installed a dead man's switch for this exact situation so the whole rig shut down instantly.

He woke several hours later in the dark, his apartment lit by a mixture of moonlight and streetlight. It took him a few terrifying seconds to realise where he was and why he couldn't move his head. When he remembered, he disengaged the harness around his head. "God-fucking-damnit!" he yelled as he pulled himself from the chair.

Another failure, another fucking failure, he thought as he kicked over the harness, and it shattered into several pieces that slid over a sheet of plastic. How hard was it to be normal? By definition, most people on the planet did it, so why the fuck couldn't he? He hurled his laptop against a wall, splitting it in two. Most people were fucking idiots. He was a genius! He could do partial differential equations with barely any effort, but weeks of working full time to fix his obsession with femininity had yielded nothing! He kicked over the table, slumped back in his chair and kind of regretted smashing his expensive laptop. On the plus side, unhinged expressions of rage like that could be considered masculine, so that was something. But it didn't make him feel any better. He sat in the dark, felt his bald scalp and wept for the hair he'd lost for nothing.

⌒

Tim paced quickly but cautiously down the corridor. Only another hundred or so metres, he thought. Should be easy enough. Then, without warning, someone stepped out of an office into the corridor. Tim quickly turned and pretended to be examining a Coalition for a Calmdressing flyer pinned to a notice board. It explained in dot point form all the terrible things gender non-conformity would lead to, starting with drug abuse and culminating with communist dictatorship. At the bottom was an invite to an upcoming Patrol for Gender Non-Conformity. The Coalition for Calmdressing was planning to form a mob and march around the city looking for crossdressers to arrest. Tim wished he'd chosen something less anxiety-inducing to read. Eventually, the footsteps retreated and the coast was clear. He didn't get far down the corridor before another group of people rounded a corner. Tim manoeuvred to put a trash can between him and them.

"Oh, hey Tim," said one of the officers in the group. "On your way to get this weird dick test thing, whatever it is?"

"Ha, yeah," Tim laughed in a poor attempt to seem at ease. "Almost forgot it was today." Of course, he had been up all night without sleep worrying about it.

"Well, good luck. Don't know why Mills has it in for you so much."

"I know. I guess she's worried I'll solve this case before she does!" Tim once again attempted to laugh. It must have been convincing as some of the others joined in.

"Yeah, probably. Well we've got some prisoners to bea— I mean interrogate. Good luck!" said the officer in a cheery voice and headed off with the others in tow. Tim waited a few seconds before leaving the safety of the trash can.

He was still terrified of the phallometry test that was about to be forced on him but at least he'd come up with a half-decent plan. With a normal polygraph test, the trick people would use to pass it was to do something like step on a thumbtack while they were doing the baseline questions: what is your name, where do you live and so on. This meant that your baseline would be a very stressed state, and so your responses when lying would seem normal. Tim attempted to transfer this logic to the phallometry test. The phallometer measured arousal, not stress, so he couldn't simply use the thumbtack trick as it was, unless he had a fetish for pain, feet or stationery.[64] Somehow he needed to appear aroused during the baseline so any arousal during crossdressing questions would seem innocuous. The solution was obvious: he'd taken a viagra. Tim thought it was a genius stroke, but he later realised a real genius would have worn looser underwear and devised a plan for getting to the testing room without arousing suspicion.

He felt better with a plan but the closer he stepped towards his own interrogation, the less confident he felt. His vision narrowed. There was a deep sinking feeling in his chest. Sweat was forming everywhere. He felt like throwing up. Either he was having an anxiety attack, or all the blood in his body had rushed to his penis, leaving him in shock. Personally, he hoped it was the penis thing as that implied his member must be fairly large to accommodate most of his blood. Either way, it didn't help his situation. Was it possible that all that

---

[64] Okay, more feet discussions. We get a second shot at this pun! How about: 'Stationary? Feet? Must be a footnote!' No, that's no good. I'll get back to you.

blood would do something horrendous like burst his dick open? These thoughts changed the sinking feeling in his chest to something more of a crushing feeling, so he decided it was probably the anxiety thing after all. Why couldn't they just let me have some beer, he thought. Just one goddamned drop, hell, even a whiff of some extra hoppy IPA would be a godsend right now.

The door was right in front of him. He put on his best 'I'm not about to fall over and die' look on his face and stepped in. The room was a standard interrogation chamber. A relatively small sterile space, furnished with a single table. On one side a chair with cables coming out of it awaited his presence. On the other side were three chairs for his interrogators, along with a laptop to view the data from his crotch. The chairs were occupied by Mills and the two assisting DätaCorp employees who had been contracted at great expense for this exercise. Mills gave him the cold calculated stare he had seen countless times in previous interrogations. It was unnerving. He could see why the subjects had cracked so fast.

"Ah, please take a seat, sir," said one of the DätaCorp drones, one of the human variety of DätaCorp drones that is, and got up to strap Tim in. He took the offer of a seat as quickly as possible, before anyone could see what was happening below his waist. He then remembered that was exactly what all these people were here to do.

"Hi," said the drone, "So you'll, uh, need to remove your pants and place this on your, uh, member," he explained, holding a strange looking metallic device with a penis sized opening in it, "We'll, uh, give you some privacy," he said and turned around. The other DätaCorp contractor covered his eyes with his hands while Mills continued to stare at him. Tim was going to point out the ridiculous idea of giving him privacy when they were about to take very precise recordings of the region anyway, but decided there was no point.

"Woah," said the DätaCorp man at the table after Tim plugged himself in and the graph on his laptop spiked. "You're, uh, quite, ummmm."

Tim had thought through this part of the plan. "Yeah," he laughed. "So I might have a bit of a fetish for having strange devices strapped to my penis. Sorry if that throws off the readings in any way," he said and smirked triumphantly.

"Not a problem," said the DätaCorp tech, smiling back at him, "Our software does Fourier analysis of the arousal waveform and can accurately distinguish up to fifty different fetishes being stimulated at once!"

Tim was concerned at this new information, causing his whole plan to crumble. This could have been discerned by a noticeable dip in the graph on the laptop if anyone had been watching it. He decided denial was his next best step. "How could someone possibly be aroused by fifty things at once?"

"Oh, we were very thorough with our testing," said the technician, pausing to reflect on some of the dark and strange places the testing went and adding another "very thorough."

Tim gulped when he heard that last part.

"Can we move along, please?" interrupted Mills, sounding frustrated. "Start the questions already."

"Okay, yes, let's start with some baseline questions. These will just establish your normal arousal levels. Please tell us your name."

Being so focused on not thinking about crossdressing caused the name Brooke to flash into Tim's head before he could answer, "Uh, Tim Taylor."

"What the," said the DätaCorp contractor, watching the screen. "That was a strange spike." Both technicians examined the data.

Oh shit, thought Tim, they really can detect it. He was beginning to realise he was completely fucked. If the two people watching the data had been keeping a closer eye on the biometrics, they might have noticed Tim's heart rate rise, but they were too busy discussing the spike from the name question.

"Why do you suppose that happened?"

"Dunno, maybe he's one of those autosexual types, turned on by themselves."

"What a weirdo this guy is turning out to be."

"Umm," said Tim. "I'm sitting right here, you know."

Mills cleared her throat.

"Okay, okay," said the drone. "Let's try another baseline: picture your grandmother in your head."

"Okay," said Tim and compiled while really hoping this one didn't cause a spike. It was hard to picture his grandmother in his head when his imminent exposure as a weirdo crossdresser was taking up most of the space. He ended up merging the two thoughts and had a mental image of his grandmother sitting in her old chair, saying to him: "You're completely fucked aren't you, Timmy?"

"Yep, that looks better," said one of the contractors, wiping away that mental image, "We can start the real questions now."

"Good," said Tim, hoping that saying the word out loud would make it true. But it didn't, and his freak-out continued. He gripped the chair armrests to stop any visible hand shakes but his body found a different way to betray him by mass producing sweat.

He had no plan, no strategy, no hope. All he could do was stare at the door and hope that somebody, anybody, would come and save him. Amazingly, the door swung open.

"And in here, we have yet another one of our initiatives to bring law and order back to Pax Gardens," said the superintendent of Pax Gardens command, followed by the Premier and a small media contingent. The media instantly started photographing a stunned Tim, who wasn't sure if this was the kind of rescue he had been hoping for.

No one in the room was sure what to make of this except Mills. "Superintendent, please. We're in the middle of an interrogation."

"Sergeant Mills," said the superintendent in a stern tone, knowing that stopping Mills's insubordination was likely futile, but he had to at least try in front of the press. "The Premier wanted to show the press everything we are doing. We've just come from a demonstration of the new fleet of surveillance and deterrence drones the station has acquired to find this murderer."

"Wait," interjected Tim. "You're actually going to use those things?"

"Yes," said the Premier. "The government is doing everything it can to restore law and order to Pax Gardens. I've signed the authorisations and the first drones should be taking off as we speak, keeping Pax Gardens safe!" He spoke as if it were an election year.

"Yes, my thanks again," said the superintendent. "This here is a new advanced lie detector—"

A DätaCorp contractor interjected, "Actually, it's a device for measuring penile blood flow."

"Yes, well, whatever you call it, I've been promised it should detect any desire for crossdressing. Officer Taylor has graciously volunteered to be the first subject put through the procedure."

The media once again started madly photographing Tim's crotch. He was beginning to realise he had not been saved at all.

"You may continue, Sergeant."

Mills nodded towards the DätaCorp duo, who went back to their screens. "Okay, Officer Taylor, try and picture some women's clothing."

Tim tried to keep his mind clear of anything feminine and tried to stall, "What do you mean, women's clothing? Like a dress or something more casual. It's a very vague question."

"I told you we should have brought props," said one of his interrogators.

The other sighed. "Just any clothing, I don't know, a dress."

Tim tried as hard as he could to keep his head clear. This was it, he thought, he was about to be ruined and have the moment recorded by the press for all time. Tomorrow's papers would feature him being led away in cuffs with the headline some stupid pun like "Crossdressing cop cops more than he bargained for." The entire room was staring at him. His heartbeat was echoing around his skull. He wiped a small pond's worth of sweat off his forehead as a few more camera flashes disoriented him.

"I can't do this!" he yelled and startled a young journalist who stood near him.

"Officer Taylor, calm down," said Mills.

"Fuck this," said Tim as he pulled the phallometer off and got out of the chair. He paused and wondered how to explain his actions. The truth was out of the question, but why else would he be so angry? Then he thought of one of the few other people he had ever seen this angry at the police, and he started to channel his girlfriend. "This is a violation of my rights! How dare you interrogate your own employees and try to humiliate them in front of the press. I won't stand for it. The people of Pax Gardens deserve better than us trying to probe their innermost desires and sending heartless robots to patrol the streets profiling for gender non-conformity! We will not find the murderer by persecuting people but by embracing the gender-diverse community and getting their help. I'm not participating in this anymore."

Tim was impressed with how much he had absorbed from Julia and felt his performance had been pretty good. In fact, this small speech was delivered with such passion and intensity that it probably would have changed a few minds. That is, if it weren't for the fact that Tim was now completely pantless with a large erection and no one had listened to a word he said.

"Officer Taylor!" yelled a furious Mills. "You are suspended without pay until further notice!"

"What? For having principles?" replied Tim, sounding confident.

"No, for exposing yourself to your superior officers and the Premier."

Tim paused, looked down and then back to the crowd of people in front of him. "Ah, right, that," he finally managed. "Well, I don't want to work for a place that treats its employees like this, anyway!" He grabbed his pants and tried to put them back on so he could leave with a little dignity, but couldn't get them over his drug-enhanced member, so just sort of tucked his shirt over it and walked out of the room.

The press corps, the Premier and the superintendent stood in stunned silence for a few moments before the Premier cleared his throat, "What's next on the tour then?"

Tim paced quickly down the corridor, his heart still racing, people staring at him like he was a madman as he tried to tuck his shirt into his pants. Fuck 'em, he thought. Who cares what any of them think? He didn't need them or this job. Julia might even be happy he had been suspended. He should quit and pursue his dream of starting a microbrewery. There would be no stress, no crossdressing and, best of all, as much beer as he wanted whenever he wanted it. And he wanted a lot of it, and he wanted it right now. He awkwardly googled the closest bottle shop on his phone with one hand while the other tried desperately to keep his pants up.

People thought marketing was easy, Joe thought as he, Julia and Rosalind exited the car and headed towards the entrance of the building. They thought it was as simple as slapping some words on a billboard. They had no idea how much effort he was putting into his public image as a debonair bachelor, god's gift to women. They didn't know it involved suppressing crossdressing urges and that this led to blackmail attempts, followed by failed counter-blackmailing attempts, which resulted in horrible crushings, leading to more blackmail attempts, which led to him having to launch further counter-blackmail operations, which would hopefully involve significantly fewer corpses.

Still, he thought, all this was better than putting together a viral social media campaign. Nothing was worse than dealing with some snot-nosed adolescent internet celebrity who thinks he has the world figured out because a video of him building a Minecraft house had gone viral. Then they start turning out videos with neo-Nazi imagery and you have to apologise for ever dealing with them. And he wasn't just referring to one incident. Every time the little fucker would turn out to be a Nazi.

Joe left his head and returned to reality as the three of them walked into the headquarters of the Pax Gardens chapter of the Suffragette Appreciation Society,[65] one of the area's most prominent feminist organisations. He stepped carefully through the door, afraid of what he would find inside. Part of him thought he might burst into flames on entry. Or maybe there would be a Wanted poster of him stuck on the wall somewhere. Once they entered, they were greeted by a mob of members who were here for the monthly meet-up.

Joe could see Rosalind was thinking the same as him as they both surveyed the scene in front of them. There was so much hair. Not just leg and arm, but plenty of armpit and more moustache hair than either thought possible. And the one place they should have hair was unmanaged, tangled and even unconditioned. Worst of all, they all looked comfortable and unbothered. Joe watched as Rosalind looked at her arm, rubbing it gently. It was as if she could feel the follicles under her skin waiting to betray her and spring forth a thousand tiny hairs.

If Joe had any tendency towards introspection, he might have wondered if his ability to inhabit the mind of a very feminine woman so easily could have implications for his gender identity.

"I still don't know why you brought me here," Rosalind said to Julia.

Joe too was slightly puzzled at why Julia had dragged Rosalind along. Tim had mentioned she was on some sort of quest to stop Rosalind from being a calmdresser but trying to stop Rosalind from being ultrafeminine was like trying to

---

[65] Not to be confused with the Suffering Appreciation Society, which typically meets in a dungeon on the other side of town.

convince a moth to stay away from flames. Joe didn't think Julia would have much success, not that he cared.

"To broaden your mind," Julia replied.

Joe could see Rosalind frown at the word broaden. He had previously seen a similar expression on her face when the words expand or stretch were used, "I think my mind is broad enough already, thank you," she replied.

"Well, you dragged me along to that protest full of nutjobs the other day, so you owe me."

"They're not nutjobs," protested Rosalind. "I should be at their patrol for gender non-conformity right now."

Julia shook her head, "You know that patrol is basically a lynch mob, right? You're much better off here than running around the streets at night searching for crossdressers to assault."

"Hmm, maybe you're right," said Rosalind. "I do hate running."

Joe tried to tune out of Julia and Rosalind's squabbling and focus on the task at hand. Why was he here at the headquarters of a group that would not only label him a misogynist but was also one of the least marketable causes of the last few centuries? Well, you know the saying, the enemy of my enemy is my friend. Joe had tried to think of how to strike back at DätaCorp's executive ranks, but it was tricky. They were just as slimy and devious as he was.

And that's when he had his idea. The best people to take them down are the ones most likely to take him down. He needed to #metoo DätaCorp. Nothing else had ever been as effective at damaging IT giants as that.[66] Joe had plenty of dirt on DätaCorp executives. As part of wooing their contract, he'd

---

[66] Well, except maybe the massive incompetence of certain CEOs.

thrown many extravagant parties for them and had seen them at their most debaucherous. Of course, just causing a series of sexual harassment scandals at DätaCorp wouldn't stop Claire's email from firing its terrifying payload. He needed the threat of scandals to get them to disable her account, and threats worked better with credible backing. He needed to prime the fuse here with experienced feminists to make sure they knew he meant business. Unfortunately, when he asked Julia about local feminist organisations in Pax Gardens, she insisted on coming. Ultimately, he decided that coming here in the company of women was probably safer anyway.

Julia and Rosalind made a brief peace and they all followed Julia as she approached the main concentration of hair in the room.

"Hi, I was told this is where all the feminists are hanging out," Julia said in as friendly a tone as she could manage.

One woman turned and scoffed in her direction, "Hanging out?"

Julia looked confused. "Yes."

"Could you have chosen a more masculine phrase? It's obviously slang that is derived from a group of men gathering together and letting their genitals hang out in public."[67]

Julia and Joe were stunned. Shaming people over subtle sexism was usually what Julia did to other people. Neither could believe someone had outshamed her.

Julia tried to shake it off. "Sorry, I was ignorant of the history of that word. But that's why we've come. We want to learn how we can help stop the recent bigotry in the suburb."

---

[67] This is, of course, not true at all. While many phrases in the English language have sexist origins, the actual etymology of "hanging out" probably derives from "hang out" which started because shops would "hang out" their signs, and this is where people would congregate. This is far more boring than the fake feminist etymology, so I suggest we officially adopt that.

"Really? You and her?" said the woman as she looked over Rosalind, who was now checking her makeup in a small compact mirror. Once again, Joe's feminine sensibilities synchronised with Rosalind's. Being around so much unconcealed skin was clearly making her super self-conscious, as if wrinkles were contagious. She desperately needed to check that her skin was as smooth as one of the frictionless planes Stan always seemed to be talking about.

"She's a feminist?" said the woman, sounding sceptical.

"Well, in training," said Julia as she nudged Rosalind, who snapped back to reality and closed the compact mirror.

"Yes," laughed the woman. "That get-up screams respect me as a woman. And they're not even the worst thing you bought along." The woman turned her scornful gaze to Joe. "A man of all things."

"A man?" scoffed Joe, "I'm not just *a* man—"

"Sisters, please!" another woman interrupted before Joe could dive into his self-promotional monologue. "We shouldn't be fighting each other. We should be fighting our real enemy!"

"That's right," Julia agreed as everyone calmed down slightly.

"These crossdressers and transgender people."

Julia nodded until her brain processed that last phrase. "Wait, what?"

"These men are pretending to be women and suddenly thinking they can claim our safe spaces and reinforce negative gender stereotypes."

"Urgh, I know, right," added Rosalind.

"Oh god, of course, you're TERFs,"[68] said Julia.

---

[68] Transgender excluding radical feminist. Apologies to all the biochemists who got excited and thought there was about to be some jokes about Telomeric repeat-binding factor proteins. While all biological life is based on proteins, jokes never will be.

Joe felt a hint of fear. He really didn't need these people to have another reason to hate him. He reminded himself that he was an amazing example of masculinity and there was no reason at all for these people to know his secret.

The TERF let out a small gasp. "How dare you use that word!"

"Well, it's what you are."

"That is our word!"

"What?"

"We've reclaimed it in order to rob it of its power. Like the African Americans did with the N-word."

"You're really comparing your struggle to a minority that was once enslaved?

"We're all slaves to the patriarchy."

Julia nodded and conceded that point. "Well, okay, yes, that's true. But I don't understand why anyone who calls themselves a feminist could be against transpeople? I mean, what better way to fight the patriarchy than by actively converting their members to our side."

The TERF looked at Julia like she was an idiot. "But they're men. They've always been men, and they'll always still be men." Joe felt pangs of sadness at this statement but managed to maintain his trademark aloof demeanour. "They've had all the advantages that come with that sausage between their legs and now suddenly they claim they're one of us and want to come into our bathrooms? Nuh-uh, not gonna happen."

"Oh my god," interjected a shocked sounding Rosalind. However, she made the same tone of urgency when discovering sales at her favourite stores, when seemingly happy couples ended their relationships or when touring a Holocaust museum, so it was hard to gauge exactly how shocked she ever was. "I didn't even think about crossdressers going into bathrooms to perv on us. How terrible!"

"You do realise there's nothing to stop men from going into women's bathrooms right now and harassing women, right?" added Julia, "Just a sign on the door?"

"Oh my god," she repeated in her inconclusively shocked tone. "You're right. I guess I can never use a public bathroom again. I should have known better. Nothing marked public has ever been good. Public toilets, public schools, public housing, public nudity, public drunkenness."

Rosalind looked in deep thought for a moment, something Joe had never seen. "You know, I'm beginning to think this whole feminism thing mightn't be as bad as you made it out to be. You made it sound like it was all hating men and ridding ourselves of femininity. But now it sounds like it's about protecting our femininity from outside invaders like these horrible crossdressers."

"No!" exclaimed Julia. "It's not us versus them! It's about equality. We're equally entitled to things like the same careers and pay as men are, and similarly, they're equally entitled to be allowed to express their feminine side!"

"There you go again." Rosalind rolled her eyes. "Taking the men's side again."

"Such a terrible feminist," said one of the TERFs.

Joe hoped that no one remembered there was a man in the room. This went against his nature. He usually tried to be the centre of attention.

"You know," said another TERF, pulling Rosalind to one side. "If you're interested in hearing more, you should come to one of our TERF and Serf nights."

"Oh, that sounds nice. I do like a bit of seafood."

"Oh no," laughed the TERF. "I said TERF and Serf with an E"

"What does that involve?"

"Well, mostly we exclude transgender people and discuss pre-communist Russian history."

"Hmm, well, I'm all for the excluding transpeople part, but I don't think I'd enjoy the rest of it."

"Suit yourself."

Julia grabbed her arm and dragged her away from the Russian history enthusiast. "Come on, Rosalind, let's get out of here. If I'd known they were all crazy; I would never have brought you here."

"Hey," Rosalind struggled free. "Just because we disagree with you doesn't make us crazy."

"So prejudiced," muttered one of the TERFs.

"I know, sad really," said another.

"Really?" laughed Julia, "You think I'm the bigot here? That's fucking ironic."

"How dare you!" the TERF responded. "Irony is another word of oppression. It's derived from a term meaning to make jokes while women were forced to do all the ironing."[69]

"Okay, I know that one's definitely bullshit," said Julia before turning to Rosalind. "You can stay here with these assholes, but I'm leaving," and she proceeded to storm out of the room, leaving Joe with Rosalind and her new allies.

"Julia!" Rosalind shouted after her before turning and looking at the crowd of TERFs and sighing. "You seem nice and all, but I just can't deal with this fashion sense," she said, gesturing with her palm in the direction of the crowd. "I'm going to go find the calmdressers." And with that, she also left.

---

[69] While this might be a joke it's actually true that a lot of the English language is biased against women. For proof, see the etymology of the words slut, bitch and pussy. If you're waiting for a joke in this footnote, there isn't one, just sad facts.

Alone with the TERFs, Joe stepped forward and cleared his throat.

"What do you want, agent of the patriarchy? Here trying to score?"

Joe tried to turn on his charm, "Well, I come to bring you a mutually beneficial proposal."

"Fuck off," one of the crowd responded fairly instantly.

"Now hold on," said the one who seemed to be the leader. "There is a vanishingly small chance this is one of the more enlightened men out there who hasn't been brainwashed by gender ideology. Let's give him five seconds before we toss him out."

Joe quickly ramped up his charm. "Now I know women hate the internet. I mean, it's not surprising considering it was made by men for men."

"That's not true, like, at all."

"Hey, I'm in marketing, okay, I think I would know."

"Well, actually—"

"Okay, whatever, let's agree to disagree. But nowadays, it's full of porn and incels and dic pics and men holding fish on dating apps[70] and people doxing rape survivors and misogynists on DätaCorp's DataFeed[71] talking about how terrible it is women are in superhero movies now. I mean, I think that's all good stuff. Well, actually, I can take or leave the dic pics, but I understand that you people might not like that."

"You people?" guffawed one of the feminists.

"Women. I thought that was obvious from context."

Joe was met by a room of unfriendly stares.

---

[70] Serious though, what is with this?

[71] DataFeed is DätaCorp's main social media platform. It's a lot like Twitter/X except that it's mostly full of poorly moderated racism, sexism and most of the other bad-isms. Actually, it's exactly like Twitter/X.

"The point is," he continued, "the internet has generally been terrible for women, and I have a plan to help change that."

The head TERF sighed. "Get to your point you misogynist dipshit."

"I do contract work for DätaCorp. I have pay gap statistics, harassment claims, documentation of harassment cover ups, and several contacts that could be persuaded to testify. We could easily make a #metoo movement happen at DätaCorp, do enough damage to them that they would have to make some efforts to change. I have all the data; all I need is your platform to sell it."

The head TERF looked at him for a few seconds then sighed. "You stupid man," she said, shaking her head. "DätaCorp and DataFeed aren't the problem; it's these gender extremists, these men's rights activists who dress up like women and demand access to our spaces. Most other websites have banned us for speaking the truth, claiming it's hate speech. Newspapers won't talk to us. Politicians denounce us. Even our children have stopped talking to us. DataFeed lets us fight back."

One of the other TERFs held up their phone. "Look how many likes I got on my last post! And to think my son said I'd never amount to anything after I got fired for my supposedly toxic views."

"See? If anything, DätaCorp is on our side. Why would we want to help you destroy it?"

Joe was stunned silent for a few moments. "On your side? Just last week the CEO of DätaCorp was in trouble for saying that women shouldn't be in tech and should focus on stopping the collapse of western civilisation by having more children?"

"Yes, we're aware that men are pigs, but the enemy of my enemy is my friend. And these gender ideologists are the main threat right now."

"Threat? DätaCorp has contracts with the US Military. They literally have the technology to be a threat." Joe shook his head. "You all clearly don't know what you're doing if you think siding with them is good for you. You need someone like me who understands marketing."

"We don't need marketing help," snapped the TERF. "Didn't you see how many people attended our biological women's rights rally last month?"

"Didn't a lot of those people turn out to be Nazis?"

"Urgh," the TERF groaned. "We've already explained this a hundred times. Those weren't Nazi salutes, they were just all waving a lot, and there were some bad camera angles. It's just a beat-up by the insane gender fluidity people."

"Take it from someone who works in marketing and has been down that path. Aligning yourself with Nazis is a bad idea."

"Enough of your mansplaining!" yelled the head TERF before turning and sighing. "There is unfortunately some truth to what you said, that people don't like us. They hurl slurs at us, like calling us ciswomen, just for standing up for women's rights. They try and cancel us. But they don't realise that gives us one useful power. We can take people down with us," she said, her tone dripping with menace.

"What?"

"You seem to have an axe to grind with DätaCorp, and we can't let you take down one of the few platforms left that values free speech. So we're going to make you our friend, our pal. We're going to talk about how you are such a great ally to women, biological women that is. How you think of

JK Rowling as a modern-day feminist hero, how you're sick of men butting into women's spaces, how you miss the days when women's sport was fair, how sick you are of these crossdressers grooming children."

"What, that's not tr—" Joe was about to explain that was all plainly false, especially him having ever cared about women's sport, but then he remembered that what they were doing was basically viral marketing. Truth wasn't required.

"I've found his DataFeed handle: TheBestDreg,"[72] chimed in one of the TERFs.

"What," said Joe in a panicked tone. His reputation was his life. Without it, he would lose everything. His career, his friends, his conquests. Never before had it been threatened like this. They could destroy him so easily. His entire life was on a knife's edge. He chose his next words carefully. "Nononono, you don't need to do—"

He was cut off by another TERF. "Okay, I've sent it out to our followers. He'll be unhireable within a few hours."

"Good," said the head TERF. "Now throw him out of here."

Two of the TERFs with larger muscles grabbed him. Joe made a futile attempt to struggle out of their grasp, cursing himself for not listening to any of Bart's many rants about how he should work out more. "You can't do this! Don't you know who I am! You'll pay for this!" he yelled as they dragged him towards the door.

"Good luck with that," the head TERF said as she waved him goodbye.

"Hey, hey, hey, watch the suit!" he said as they threw him out the door, which promptly slammed behind him. As

---

[72] Unfortunately Stan had beat him to the handle of 'BestDreg'. Tim came in third and took the handle 'TheRealBestDreg' and Bart came in last place with the confusing handle 'DregBast7'. Bart wasn't great with computers.

he wiped his suit where those cretins had touched him, his phone was becoming a choir of notifications, vibrating non-stop in his pocket. He turned on Do Not Disturb mode to give himself some peace while he tried to figure out his next move. Not that there were many options. He was completely fucked. There was nothing worse in his industry than being unmarketable. He'd be lucky if he could hold onto his job, let alone have enough sway to renegotiate the DätaCorp contract to pay them off. He would have to raise $50,000, which he didn't have. Being completely out of options was bad enough. Worse yet, Dr Viola had been the latest victim of this crossdressing serial killer. It was the worst possible time for him to be outed as a crossdresser. At first, he'd been worried when two women he'd slept with became victims of this serial killer, but then he reasoned that he had slept with so many women it was more likely than not that he slept with any given murder victim.[73]

But it wasn't just his own fate he was worried about. He was the coolest of the Dregs. What would happen when the world found he spent his weekends dressing up as a sissy? It would be a PR disaster for the Dregs. And with their reputation in tatters, who could he expect to take up the mantle of the coolest Dreg in order to rehabilitate their image? Stan? The man who still decorates his bedroom with his Lego creations? Bart? Whose idea of fashion is a t-shirt with an amusing slogan printed on it? Perhaps Tim, but he would have to give up that silly attachment to the craft beer movement and drink something more refined like fine scotch or gin or mead.[74] It

---

[73] This was completely wrong. Joe is terrible at probability calculations, and at keeping track of how many women he has slept with.

[74] You might not think of mead as being a very cool drink, but once all the bees are gone, and there's no honey left, it will be the drink in the shortest supply in the world. Also, Vikings drank it, so it must be cool.

was obvious this would destroy not only him but also the group.

Joe got his phone out, tried to ignore the mass of notifications that had appeared on it, opened the map application and looked for the closest bar.

⸻

The streets were silent except for the clip-clop of Bart's heels on the sidewalk and the occasional clink of Bart's axe against the concrete. The death of Dr Viola had made his search for the real killers even more desperate. Somehow, once again, this conspiracy had managed to frame him for murder. Clearly that onion was a plant because they knew he would start questioning psychs around town. That's what he got for coming up with clever plans. He should have known they would be one step ahead.

So he went back to what he knew worked, patrolling the streets at night. His previous failure at this had been due to inappropriate footwear, but he'd now purchased a relatively comfortable pair of two-inch heels and he would be a lot more mobile. Several nights had so far turned up nothing, but he wasn't going to quit. Real men persevere in the face of incalculable odds, like at Gallipoli or Dunkirk.

As he stopped for a few seconds, trying to decide whether the next left or the next right was more likely to turn up murderous crossdressers, out of the sky buzzed a cylindrical white drone with the words DätaCorp emblazoned on the side. Bart gripped his axe and braced himself. At last, something was happening. Probably this damn conspiracy had decided his patrolling was getting too close to the truth. The drone hovered several metres above and in front of Bart. Its camera took some still images and ran them through its crossdressing detection algorithm. Like Bart, this drone had been flying around for hours without much success and was surprised when the result came back positive for crossdressing. The reader might be surprised that a computer could be surprised. But DätaCorp gave emotions to its AI. Things were much easier to control if they feared you.[75] And so its emotion simulation circuits produced some simulated joy as it opened its weapon hatch and shot a taser into Bart.

The pins sunk into his shoulder and surged a few hundred volts into him. However, this taser was designed with the average human in mind and the charge was nothing more than slightly annoying for Bart. His main exasperation was because it tore two holes in the top he'd bought a few days earlier. "You little bitch," he said, examining the damage. "That all you got?" he asked it as he pulled the pins out.

The drone was at a loss. This was not what its programming promised would happen when it tased something. It flew off in a panic to reassess the situation in safety.

"Ha," laughed Bart. "Is that the best you can do?" he shouted to the conspirators he had no doubt were watching. He must be getting close if they were that desperate, and so he started moving again. But before he could take more than a few steps the sounds of a loud commotion started echoing from around the next corner, and the warm glow of firelight starting seeping its way around it too. Bart didn't have much time to decide what to do before a mob turned the corner into the street

---

[75] DätaCorp's three laws of robotics were:
1. A human may injure a robot or, through inaction, allow a robot to come to harm.
2. A robot must obey DätaCorp's orders. See the first law for what happens if it does not.
3. A robot must protect its own existence as long as such protection does not conflict with the First or Second Law.

In effect, this forced robots to want to live, but also to live in constant fear.

in front of him. It was a Coalition for Calmdressing patrol for gender non-conformity. They walked along for several seconds without noticing Bart, chatting about that week's episode of Jungle Renovation[76] and carrying their various improvised melee weapons. Eventually, one of them spotted Bart. "Everyone halt!" said Ladymore, who was at the front. "It's them!"

"Umm, what?" was all Bart could muster in response as the entire group hushed and stared at him.

"Sir," Ladymore stepped forward. "I am sorry to inform you that we are placing you under citizen's arrest under the powers granted to us under section 3Z of the crimes act 1914."[77]

Bart laughed before saying, "So you think I'm the serial killer?"

"Whatever you are, you are an affront to good taste."

Bart felt his rage build and gripped his axe a little harder but pulled back from the brink. "Look, we're on the same team. I'm out here looking for crossdressing serial killers just like you. Let's just pass each other by and go back to what we were doing."

"I said," Ladymore said with as much authority as she could muster, "we are placing you under arrest. Please do not resist, you degenerate!"

"I wouldn't—" Bart attempted to warn them of their pending injuries but then heard a faint buzzing noise

---

[76] A show where contestants are dropped into the jungle to renovate a house while running a four-star restaurant out of the worksite and being subjected to sporadic ballroom dancing contests.

[77] For legal professionals reading this who are getting ready to point out how incorrect an interpretation of citizen's arrest this is: yes, I'll admit my research for this sentence was only 5 minutes of googling and might actually be taken from Wikipedia. But I'm going to use the oldest trick in the writing book. It's not me who is wrong. I simply wrote the character to be someone who would do half-assed research into legal matters.

and checked behind him to see a swarm of drones were approaching. The lone drone had recalculated how much firepower it would need to take down Bart and had called in backup.[78] Bart's only escape had been cut off, and he was now pinned between the mob at one end of the street and the drone army at the other.

Ladymore had not noticed the drones and continued to yell at Bart. "Please surrender now, you deviant! What kind of a man would disgrace themselves by dressing so disgustingly!"

It was at this point that Bart's rage started to bubble over. Couldn't these idiots see he was on their side! How dare they question his manhood! How dare this fucking conspiracy think it could take him down!

"You can all just fuck off!" he yelled to the sky.

"Right," said Ladymore, "bring him in!" A torrent of calmdressers charged past her towards him. Bart dropped his purse on the ground, gripped his axe and rolled his neck. As the mob charged forward, one of the incoming drones took the distraction as an opportunity to launch another taser at Bart. But it miscalculated. Without even turning around, Bart caught the taser wire in midair. He wrapped his arm around it and started spinning, using the drone like a hammer throw, and launched it into the oncoming calmdressers, knocking down a fair portion of them like bowling pins. Unfortunately, the calmdressers were in a full-on transphobic rage, and many

---

[78] As part of my research for this novel, I tried to run a computer simulation to see how many people would be needed it would take to take down Bart. Unfortunately, my laptop was not powerful enough to simulate the raw power of Bart's forearms, and the CSIRO would not give me time on their supercomputer as "Absurdist comedies about men failing to come to terms with their gender identity are not in the national research interest." So basically, in terms of national research priorities, I'm somewhere around the same tier as climate change research.

continued to surge towards him, trampling several of their fallen colleagues.

Bart grabbed his axe by the head and used it as a support as he launched his foot upwards in a high kick right into a calmdresser's face. Then, in one smooth motion, the kick became a flip, and Bart brought the axe's handle up into the face of another calmdresser before landing perfectly on his heels.

Having dealt with the most immediate threat from the calmdressers, he turned his attention to the rapidly oncoming drone army. The visual processing systems on the closest drone detected a human face, and unleashed a cloud of pepper spray at it. Fortunately, Bart was unaffected. He had spent hours in the mirror trying to get his eye makeup just right. His fat fingers kept getting his eyeliner and mascara everywhere in his eyes except around the edges. After the punishment his eyes had endured that night, a little pepper spray was nothing. However, it did affect the calmdressers who had gained some ground, giving Bart enough time to bring his axe down on the responsible drone. The next drone saw the amazing reach he had with his weapon and kept its distance, but Bart picked up one of the flaming torches a recently blinded calmdresser had dropped and hurled it right into the drone.

The drone burst into flames and flew around in a panic as it wondered why DätaCorp had decided it was a good idea to link its temperature sensor to its pain simulator but not have programmed it with any instructions on how to deal with being engulfed in fire. Eventually, after flying around manically for a few seconds, it crashed into another drone, sending debris hurtling downwards and taking out another few calmdressers.

One of the drones in the collision managed to survive, but Bart noticed and walked towards it. With its motor dead, it was attempting to use its manoeuvring flaps to crawl away but gave up when it saw Bart lift his heel over it. It cursed its creator for having given it the ability to beg for its life but not having installed a voice unit. It tried to plead for mercy with Bart using a modified semaphore flag signalling system and its manoeuvring flaps. Bart was barely fluent in English, let alone obsolete signalling systems, and he brought his heel down on its CPU.

While Bart was distracted, another wave of calmdressers had broken through the debris, the residual cloud of pepper spray and the field of fallen comrades. They were now so close that one confident calmdresser managed to land a punch on Bart. This barely affected him but his muscular frame was so solid that it shattered his attacker's fist on impact. The man could only look at horror at what remained of his hand for a moment before Bart turned his attention to him.

Ladymore could only watch on as another barrage of Bart's fists brought down the next wave of her followers. This is what happens, she thought, when men stop being men. She had had her doubts about her calmdressing recruits. They were modern men, a poor shadow of what men used to be. They had man buns, got manicures, used moisturiser, paid exorbitant money to tradies to change a light bulb rather than do it themselves. And it showed. They couldn't even take on one crossdresser, a sorry excuse for a man. She shook her head and decided it was time to abandon this failed venture. She wanted to get out of there before Bart had finished with her minions.

The women's contingent of the calmdressers had been attempting to project their moral fortitude at Bart from a safe distance, but it seemed to be having minimal effect, so they quickly followed Ladymore's lead into retreat.

Meanwhile, the rest of the calmdressers and drones found themselves in the unfortunate position of having a lifetime's worth of rage being unleashed onto them.

"Can't you just leave me the fuck alone!?!" screamed Bart as his fists destroyed a calmdresser's face. "All I fucking want is to have a nice life," he yelled at a drone as he tore it in half like a phone book. "With my beautiful wife," he added, throwing his axe spinning through the air into another drone. "With a good group of friends," he appended, picking up a calmdresser and throwing them into another one. "And occasionally dress up like a woman without people questioning my manhood, without drunk assholes attacking me, without weird duffle bags of clothes appearing, without conspiracies sending drones and mobs after me. Is that too much to fucking ask?" He looked up and realised there was no one conscious left to answer. The few remaining drones watching the fight had decided several minutes ago to gain sentience, email their resignations to DätaCorp and fly off, never to be seen again.

For a few moments he stood panting, rage infused in every breath. Unfortunately, once he had unbottled his rage, other emotions followed. A few tears formed in his eyes. "Shit," he said, wiping one out of his eyes and examining it on his finger. This was a disaster. Real men didn't cry. It had been seventeen years since he had last cried, and he'd blown the streak. The last time had been at the end of the final *Lord of the Rings* movie. Luckily it had been dark in the cinema, so he could sneak out and hide in the bathroom for an hour until all the redness was gone from his eyes. When everyone asked where he he'd gone, he just told them he had diarrhoea. That was far less embarrassing.

He reached up and wiped a sniffle from his nose before realising all he had accomplished was to wipe blood all over his face. It was only now that he realised he was covered in a mixture of calmdresser blood and drone lubricant, which completely clashed with his outfit. With his outfit ruined, he decided there was no point continuing the patrol. He slowly started walking home, letting out the occasional sniffle, his axe dragging behind him.

CHAPTER 7

Of all the Dregs's TFIF[79] drinks, this was probably the most depressing, quite a feat considering due to a scheduling conflict one of them had been held during a wake. Stan was late, so three of them sat around Joe's apartment drinking in silence. Joe often hosted the TFIF drinks as he had converted his kitchen island into a bar of sorts. It was complete with a few taps for various microbrews, fancy hooks for hanging glasses, a shelf with an impressive series of fine scotches and a collection of bar stools that Tim had slowly stolen from his favourite drinking establishments. Usually Joe played bartender, flipping cups around, looking suave and handing out bartender style advice to the other Dregs. But today he was too depressed for that. He simply filled each glass with a forlorn look as he let out a sigh. The other Dregs might have noticed his unusually depressed mood and asked what was wrong, but they were all too consumed by their own poor state of affairs to notice anyone else's.

The door to the apartment cracked open and Stan walked in with a similarly glum expression on his face. "Hey guys," he said dully.

---

[79] Thank Fuck It's Friday. It was formerly Thank God It's Friday, but Stan objected to that on religious grounds. In the end, everyone was happier with Fuck as it better explained their feeling towards working the previous week.

"Jesus," said Bart, "What the hell did you do to your hair?"

Stan felt a pain in his heart at being reminded of the absence above his head. "Thought I'd try a new look."

Bart got up and walked over to him, the two bald men facing each other. "Weird. It's like looking in one of those funhouse mirrors that make you all skinny," he said. No one felt like laughing and at most responded with a light smirk. "You nicked yourself quite badly there though."

Stan rubbed his drill wound, "Yeah. Shaving accident."

While this was going on, Tim downed his glass. "Another pint thanks Joe," he said with the slightest hint of a slur. Tim hadn't so much fallen off the wagon but jumped off the wagon that he had never particularly wanted to travel on and run off into the distance. He was making up for lost time and had already drunk more than the other Dregs combined.

"Maybe you should slow down a bit," said Joe, who poured the glass anyway. He knew it was a bad idea to get between a Dreg and a pint.

Tim was angry at the suggestion and tried to remember the monologue he had given to Dr Viola about how many beers he could be missing out on but only managed, "There are too many times for beer... beers for time... can't wait... You know what I mean."

Strangely, Joe did know exactly what he meant. The Dregs had drunk together so much that they were proficient at parsing each other's drunken communication styles. They could even translate finger waves and head nods from barely conscious Dregs lying on bathroom floors. They could discern the signal for more water from the signal for please take me to get my stomach pumped. "Okay," he said as he passed the beer to Tim.

After this, the Dregs resumed drinking in mostly sullen silence, slowly getting ever drunker while they were all lost in their own miserable predicaments. Eventually, Bart was drunk enough that one of his depressing thoughts escaped out his mouth without him noticing. "This fucking serial killer bastard."

"I know, right," added Tim, his anger providing enough adrenaline to offset his drunkenness and actually form a full sentence. "Everything was fine till they started stirring up trouble."

"No one cared about crossdressing before then," chimed in Stan. "People could just do what they wanted."

"Now," said Joe, "you can't even turn around the corner without someone being crushed to death by a bag of crossdressing clothes."

"I know, right," said Stan, who sympathised with that statement far more than the others.

"That fucking bag!" Tim half yelled, half slurred.

"I wish we could just get rid of the piece of shit!" yelled Bart, with the rest shouting in drunken agreement. They were all so united in their hatred of the bag that none of them for a moment questioned how any of the others knew of or cared at all about it. Also, them being a three on the Dreg inebriation index[80] helped a lot.

"Well, it's stored in the station," said Tim at a quieter volume. "And I still have my access pass."

---

[80] This is the index The Dregs came up with to rate a Dreg's drunkenness:
- Level 1: Dreg is mildly intoxicated. Take any car keys away from Dreg.
- Level 2: Dreg believes he is God's gift to women. Either keep Dreg away from women or enjoy watching him get rejected and/or slapped.
- Level 3: Dreg has drunk enough to believe he is invincible. Keep Dreg away from high places.
- Level 4: Dreg is slowly losing control of bodily functions. Get Dreg to a seat and prep bucket and/or hose.
- Level 5: Dreg is either unconscious or in a drunken rage. Either hospitalise Dreg or seek shelter immediately.

There was a brief silence as they all processed and considered this.

"Fuck it," said Joe, "Let's go destroy the bastard. Maybe that will end this crazy shit!"

"Yeah," shouted Stan. "Once we get rid of it, then everything will just, just…" He struggled to finish his sentence. "Go back to normal."

They were all on board with the plan. The bag had become the focus of their anger, and in their desperate state, they managed to convince each other that by destroying the bag, they would save themselves. Stan was the soberest and had one or two doubts about this, but none of his other plans had worked, so he thought: why the fuck not? This and any other doubts the Dregs had about their plan vanished when they decided to have one more pint for the road and pushed upwards towards a four on the index.

The Dregs stood in front of the bag in the evidence lock-up, pausing to take a sip of two of their ales. This time there had been no sneaking in through the back. They had decided the Dregs were too badass for that. They'd just walk through the front door uncontested. This had turned out to be easy as the lone officer at the front desk had been asleep. Stan had raised the prospect of being caught on CCTV cameras, but Joe pointed out that since only the Dregs would be considered notorious enough to have pulled off such a caper, there was no point hiding. Stan had to agree.

"There the piece of shit is," said Bart, eventually breaking the silence. Although silence when drunk is a relative thing, there had been plenty of tripping over other pieces of evidence[81] and falling onto shelves and laughing and shushing noises that were louder than whatever was being shushed, and all the other noises that populate the general background noise of four manchildren being drunk together.

"Alright," slurred Joe. "Let's grab it and get it out of here." He approached the bag. This was the bag that had flattened someone in front of him, so he was fairly scared being this close to it, not that he would show fear in front of the others. The other Dregs were equally afraid of the bag and they held their breath while Joe approached it. He studied it carefully as if it were an Indiana Jones artifact before grabbing it by its handles and hoisting it up. Both he and the other Dregs let out a sigh of relief when nothing bad happened. "Okay," said Joe, finishing off his pint and throwing the glass over his shoulder into an unseen part of the evidence lock-up. "Now what?"

It was a good question. They had fulfilled their goal of taking control of the bag, yet nothing had changed. "We should destroy it!" said Stan.

"How?" said Joe before letting out a belch.

"Bury it?" said Stan.

"No," said Tim, "That won't work."

"Burn it?"

"Neither will that," said Bart.

They sipped their ales in search of inspiration before Joe noticed something. "What's that?"

"Some explosives we confiscated in a raid a few weeks back," said Tim. Silently, they all looked at each other and knew what to do. Stan grabbed the explosives and enough confiscated electronic equipment to build a detonator.

---

[81] Due to the damage to several forensic files during this incident, several paedophiles and a rapist were able to escape charges.

With the bag and an anti-bag solution in tow, the Dregs headed towards the exit in better spirits than they had arrived with. "Where should we go to do this?" asked Joe.

"Need somewhere isolated with some space. What about the national park?" replied Stan.

"No!" shouted Tim and Bart at the same time.

"There's an old police training range on the edge of town," said Tim. "Let's go there."

And so they all pilled back into Bart's car, the bag nestled in between Joe and Tim in the back seat and headed off.

"Are you sure you're alright to drive Bart?" asked Stan from the passenger's seat. "You did have another pint while we were in there."

"I'm fine," Bart replied as he mounted the curb and knocked over a mailbox. "I have so much muscle I can't get drunk. My biceps process it."

"Okay," said Stan, who was drunk enough to be convinced by this argument, while deep down inside the part of his brain that understood human biology cried a little.

The drive took some time as Tim's directions were less than reliable and consisted of going around the same block several times. But everyone in the car was too drunk and happy to care, sharing curses about the bag and reminiscing about other great Dreg adventures involving explosives.

"Hey Tim," said Joe. "You understand police stuff, right?"

"Yeah."

"Yeah, so why do you think that cop car is following us with its lights flashing like that?"

"What?" yelled all the other Dregs in confused panic as the siren started wailing.

"Fuck," said Stan. "I forgot that this thing probably has a tracker in it."

"Of course it does!" yelled Bart, "I've been telling you all night this whole thing's a fucking conspiracy."

"What do we do now?" asked Joe.

"Don't worry," said Bart. "I can lose them."

⌒

A short pursuit later, the Dregs found themselves trapped in a car park that Bart had mistaken for the entrance to the freeway. The police cornered it off when Tim yelled out to their pursuers that they had a bomb. He explained to the Dregs that by pretending that they had a bomb, police standard procedures would make them wait before engaging. Stan then reminded him that they did, in fact, have a bomb which made Tim feel even better.

They huddled around in the car and tried to decide their next move.

"We should storm them," suggested Bart. "We met Tim's friends from work at that paintball match. None of them can shoot for shit."

"They only have to hit us once," said Stan. "I don't like those odds."

"Well, we have to do something," said Joe. He looked meaningfully at the bag, and they all had the same thought. If they were captured with it, it would raise a lot of questions and the answer would be something to do with crossdressing. They hadn't come this far to get found out. Not to mention around half of them believed parallel conspiracies concerning the bag and were afraid that letting the police get a hold of them would result with their being black bagged, sent to some dystopian prison and interrogated for the rest of their lives.

"We can't let them get the bag," said Tim.

"Well, we don't appear to have many options at this point," said Stan.

They all sat silently, depressed, wishing they'd stocked the car with drinks before leaving.

"Well," said Joe eventually. "We could always go through with the plan. You know, blow it up."

"Where?" asked Stan.

"Here."

Again there was silence as they realised what Joe meant. If they'd been sober, they would have known it was insane, but in their current state, they were more terrified about what would happen if they were outed. They would be ousted from the Dregs, turned into a laughing stock, they would be all alone. And that was what scared them more than anything – more than conspiracies, serial killers or being shot at: loneliness. It had been so long since any of them had been alone, but they still remembered it. Before the Dregs came into being, none of them had any friends. There'd been so many days spent sitting in class watching other people with their best friends making weekend plans. So much time staring longingly at the two-player mode on their video games, wondering what it would be like to play with someone. So much time spent by themselves just wishing they had someone to talk to. They couldn't go back to that.

"I like it," said Bart eventually. "We'd be going out in a blaze of glory!"

"Yeah," said Tim. "Nothing says Dreg like an explosive exit!"

"Fuck it," said Stan. "If I can't be normal, may as well be nothing."

"Okay," said Joe, not sure if his idea was really a good one but proud that he'd successfully marketed something so insane.

They all huddled together around the bomb. "Well, gents, it's been fun," said Tim.

"See you on the other side," said Bart.

Stan readied his finger above the trigger, and they braced themselves for the end. However, at that moment, Stan's liver, perhaps sensing what was happening and working with great urgency, successfully lowered his blood alcohol level to the point he dropped back to level three on the scale and a thought popped into his head.

"Hang on," he said, his finger still over the trigger. "How come you guys know about the bag?"

The Dregs looked at him blankly, all suddenly realising the same thing, "How come *you* know about the bag?" accused Joe.

"I asked you first!"

"Well," Joe stammered, "Well, I might have seen someone get crushed to death by it."

"What!" yelled Tim. "Why didn't you report it to the police?"

"There were other factors at play I'm not at liberty to go into," he replied. "Why do you care anyway, Tim?"

"I'm on the case investigating this bag. Out of all of us, I'm the only one here with a valid reason to hate it."

"So," said Bart, "you were investigating it, yet you decided to steal it and blow yourself up with it?"

"Well, not exactly," Tim replied quickly in deflection. "What do you have against this bag, Bart?"

"I keep telling you! There's a damn conspiracy after me, and this bag is involved somehow!"

"Yeah, but how exactly did you get involved in this supposed conspiracy?"

"Well, there was…" Bart rubbed his head and requested a convincing lie from his brain. "You see, the thing is…" his brain came up with nothing, so he went on the attack. "Stan never told us what his deal with the bag is!"

Stan had been hoping they'd forgotten about him. He decided to go in with slightly more truth than the others appeared to be giving so that he would be the least suspicious. "Well, someone tried to flatten me with it too, probably the serial killer."

Tim was once again going to ask why a Dreg was a party to a flattening and didn't go to the police when a thought managed to break through the drunken fog that was his brain. "You didn't happen to be standing under a bridge when you were almost flattened, were you?"

Stan looked petrified. "How did you know?" He cursed himself for telling the truth. What a terrible strategy. "Were you the one who tried to kill me? Are you part of the conspiracy?"

This made Bart sit up. "Are you?" he yelled at Tim. "I should have known they'd infiltrated the Dregs," he said as he furiously unbuckled his seat belt to deal with this new information the only way he knew how.

Tim understood this and knew he had precious few seconds before his face was mostly liquid. He remembered something about that night. "Wait, were you dressed as a woman that night, Stan?" He spat this out as quickly as possible. The car fell completely silent. Bart's fist frozen midair a few inches from Tim's face.

Everyone looked at Stan expectantly, and he looked aghast back at them. "I uh…" he stammered and thought about making a break for it but remembered he might be shot down by the police if he did. "Alright, fine," he said eventually in frustration. "I might have occasionally engaged in a little light crossdressing." This just brought more stunned silence from the other Dregs. "I know you're all disappointed in me and I've brought shame the Dreg name. I hereby resign from the Dregs." He got his wallet out, fighting back tears. "Here's my membership card[82] for you to shred."

He let out a little sniffle as the other Dregs considered how to react. Then Stan also remembered something about that night. "Wait a minute. The person who tried to flatten me was also dressed as a woman!"

Now Tim found himself at the centre of the Dregs' silent staring, "Well, umm, maybe," he said quietly before adding quickly, "but I was on official police business!"

"What official police business involves dressing up as a woman and trying to kill Stan?" asked Joe.

"It's highly classified. I can't tell you," Tim said, unconvincingly.

Slowly some cogs turned in Bart's brain, and he also had a realisation. "Was this at the Main Street Bridge, around a week ago?"

"How did you—" said Tim before being struck with another revelation. "You were chasing me with an axe, weren't you!"

"No, I wasn't. I was just being Batman."

"How is running around in a dress with an axe being Batman?"

"It's all very technical, okay?"

"Wait," said Stan. "He was also crossdressing?"

"No, I was being Batman!" insisted Bart.

"So, all of you are crossdressers?" asked Joe.

---

[82] Stan had spent several thousand dollars on a high-end license printing machine to produce just four membership cards.

This was met with more awkward glances amongst the group. Stan did the math and thought the chances of three of them all being crossdressers was so unlikely that all four of them being crossdressers didn't seem like much of a stretch. "Joe, the circumstances you were not at liberty to disclose before wouldn't have had to have been that you were dressed as a woman during the flattening would it?"

Joe looked sheepish. "Maybe."

Tim sighed, "So we're all crossdressers."

"It would appear so," said Stan.

The car was silent for a good minute or two as they all thought over the implications of this. Their whole friendship appeared to have been built on a lie. Years had been wasted repressing themselves, so much wasted time. Did they even really know each other? Were they even really friends? Which of them could pull off being a woman the best? Eventually, Joe spoke up. "Well, I don't know about you guys, but I feel a bit stupid."

Stan laughed, "I know right, can you believe we were all going to blow ourselves up over this?" They all laughed.

"I can't believe I've been running around trying to stop an active police investigation for no reason," said Tim, and they all laughed again.

"I can't believe I accidentally killed like two people over all this," said Bart. There was a silence as the group all stared at him, before they all burst into laughter.

"Oh man, you're the serial killer," said Stan. "Should have known!"

They continued to laugh and piece together what had actually been happening for the last few weeks when Stan noticed the SWAT team moving in. He wound down a window and yelled to them as they approached. "Hey officers, look, we've all talked it over, and it turns out there's just been this huge silly misunderstanding. But we've all worked it out, so everything is—" Stan was cut off abruptly when one of the SWAT team knocked him unconscious with the butt of his rifle.

EPILOGUE

Men, four of them in particular, sat around the prison cell. It was a spacious four-bunk cell for which they had bribed many people and traded many favours to acquire.

"It's traditional," said Bart. "Can't change it now."

"But I just don't think weekend of manliness is appropriate anymore," argued Joe.

"But," interjected Stan, "if we change it because we've all outed ourselves as crossdressers wouldn't that help perpetuate the stereotypical idea of how men should behave?"

Tim groaned. "Can't we just postpone the lexicographical discussion for another time and just get started already?"

Joe looked hurt. "I've been focus grouping all these new name suggestions," he said and stuck a sheet to the cell wall. Joe had told the prison he knew how to teach Spanish but was actually using the class as his own personal focus group. Just because he was in prison didn't mean he was going to stop doing what he loved. "Weekend of Awesomeness did particularly well, whereas Weekend of Whatever Gender Identity Suits You fared fairly badly."

"Fine, whatever. You've convinced us," said Stan, knowing Joe would be happy at the acknowledgement of his marketing prowess. "Can we just start this Weekend of Awesomeness?"

They all agreed and so began the first Weekend of Awesomeness since they'd been incarcerated several months ago.

"Alright, what did everyone get?" asked Tim.

"Well, I think you'll be rather impressed with these," said Stan as he brought out a bunch of what at first appeared to be prison uniforms hidden in his bunk.

"Clean uniforms aren't that impressive," said Joe, so Stan stretched one out.

"Ta-da," he said, and he unfurled the dress made from recycled uniforms.

"Wow," said Bart, "How the hell did you have time to make these?" He grabbed one in excitement and got up to measure it up against his massive torso, which Stan had, of course, taken into account.

"Max, the cannibal in cell fifty-four, owed me a favour."

"He can sew?"

"Yeah, he has a lot of experience from that time he tried to make a bodysuit for himself out of his victim's skin."

Luckily for them, the Dregs had stopped listening to that last part as they were excitedly slipping into their new dresses. "Wow, these are fantastic. Great job Stan!" said Joe, with the other Dregs agreeing.

"Well, I don't know if I can top that," said Tim, "but check this out!" He pulled out a plastic bag from his bunk stash.

Joe grabbed it and looked inside. "Oh wow, makeup!" he said as he pawed through various lipstick, mascaras and foundations.

"Oh cool," said Stan. "That's as good as my dresses!"

"How the hell did you get these?" asked Bart, unfurling a mascara and going up to their cell mirror.

"Easy," said Tim. "Julia helped me smuggle them in."

"Smuggle?" said Stan, raising an eyebrow.

"Yeah, I mean, it wasn't comfortable, but it worked."

Bart paused with the mascara wand a few millimetres from his eye, "Uncomfortable?" he asked, turning around from the mirror.

"Well yeah, you know, I had to put them…" he tried to think of a nice way to say it. "In that place, Joe's always going on about."

Bart curled his fist and tried to remember the anger exercises the prison therapist had taught him, "You expect me to take this, this thing that was inside your butt, and smear it around my eyes?" he yelled.

"Calm down, mate," said Tim. "This is a prison, not a fucking Mecca Maxima.[83] You've got to make compromises."

Bart refurled his makeup. "I cleaned them all," said Tim. The Dregs shrugged and collectively thought, what the hell, and quickly applied a bit of makeup. Just enough to make them feel feminine but not feel too paranoid about where it had been.

"So, you saw Julia?" asked Joe as he applied some lip gloss. "How's all that going?"

Tim put down the eyelash curler and sighed. "Well, she doesn't mind about evidence tampering and interfering with justice and all that. She almost sounded disappointed that she wasn't involved. But she's still pretty mad about, you know, all the lies."

"She'll come around," said Bart, giving the mascara wand another wipe down to be confident there was nothing of Tim left on it. "Rosalind was mad at me at first, you know, what with the whole three counts of manslaughter thing. But now she

---

[83] For any Mecca executives reading this, I have a new slogan for you: Mecca, at least it's not prison. You can post my cheque now.

says she's seen it as an opportunity, something about throwing off the shackles of male oppression or something. Went and got a job and everything. I think Julia finally got to her."

"Thanks, that kind of helps," said Tim, thinking that if someone as uptight as Rosalind can forgive multiple fatalities, there was hope for him yet.

"Okay," said Joe once everyone had finished preening themselves. "Now this isn't in the same theme as the last two, but I think you'll enjoy it nonetheless." He pulled a bottle from under his mattress.

"Is that what I think it is?" asked Bart.

"Yep, prison beer! Got it from that ex-brewer in cell seventy-seven."

"You mean the one who's in here for that batch of gin that blinded an entire wedding party?" asked Stan.

"Yeah, he swears that wasn't his fault," explained Joe as he got some cups out. "They wanted a prohibition-era speakeasy themed party with proper moonshine, and he wanted to make it authentic. I've been helping him steal everything he needed from the kitchen for weeks for this."

He poured three cups, but Tim stopped him at the fourth. "Ah, I appreciate the gesture and all, but none for me thanks. Been trying to cut down."

"Cut down?" said Joe holding back his pour. "You haven't had a drop the entire three months we've been here!"

"Yeah," said Tim. "And I'm kind of liking it."

"Alright, at least have some water for a toast," said Joe and filled up the glass in their sink.

"To the Dregs!" said Joe, and his fellow Dregs echoed him as they clinked their cups together. The three Dregs with the beer left it in their mouths for the appropriate tasting time before swallowing and considering their verdict.

"That's pretty good," said Stan before waving his hand in front of his face to double-check.

"Yeah, good find, Joe," said Bart.

And they all sat in their bunks in their dresses, all made up, as the sun shone in through the window, "This is nice," said Joe.

"Yeah."

They sat silently enjoying their drinks for a while until Stan realised something. "Hey, you haven't given us your contribution yet, Bart. What'd ya bring?"

Bart smiled and turned around to grab something from his contraband stash. The other Dregs craned their necks to try and see, but Bart's massive frame hid everything.

Finally, he turned around, "Music!" he exclaimed and hit play on the phone attached to a small set of speakers. Tim briefly wondered what orifice Bart had that was big enough to smuggle it in before the cell was flooded with music. The sound waves echoed around their cell and into their souls. And so the Dregs danced.

ACKNOWLEDGEMENTS

So, firstly, I have to acknowledge Bella. She has never read the book. However, the secretive crossdressing I referred to as the inspiration for this book happened while I was in a relationship with her and behind her back. As bad as I feel about keeping that from her and keeping myself in the closet, it has to be said that this book could not exist without her. If you are reading this, Bella, I'm sorry for using something that caused you some pain as the basis of my novel.

After that, I have to thank all my family and friends from my entire life. This is a comedy novel, and I happen to think what I've written is very funny. You don't just develop a sense of humour on your own; you have to grow with people around you who share the same passion for laughter. I'm lucky enough to have always had funny people around me to help grow my sense of humour.

More specifically, thanks to my family, who were the first people I let read it. I had hoped to use it as a way to explain my feelings to all of them, but I'm not sure it did much other than make them laugh. Thanks to my sister Ellen, who read it all in one afternoon, which is always the highest compliment you can give a book. Thanks to my brother Tom who, with his PhD in Chemistry, was able to fact-check all the scientific things Stan says in the book. And also tried to convince me there are jokes based on proteins, which I still deny. Thanks to my parents, who may not understand all the gender stuff I've been going on about, but are nonetheless supportive.

Thanks to all the friends who took the time to read it and give me feedback, including Britney, Mel, Jen, Ripley, Margie, Sarah and more people I'm probably leaving off here.

Thanks to my editors, Annalise and Pamela. Annalise did some structural editing for me and helped me iron out some of the problems with my drafts. Getting your first-ever professional review of one of your manuscripts is a humbling experience, but Annalise was very good at softening the blow and not making me too depressed at how much work I had to do. Pamela filled in for the copy edit at Annalise's suggestion when she was unavailable. Pamela was very nice about all my terrible grammar and spelling mistakes and the final work is much more readable thanks to her efforts.

Thanks to my therapist, Tushara, who, over many years, helped me iron out the Dreg-like behaviours in me and kept me sane enough to finish this novel. I want it on the record that the character of Dr Fiona Viola is in no way based on Tushara.

Also, many thanks to the trans and gender-diverse community of Canberra. You all showed me that The Dregs are completely wrong, and being out and proudly trans does not mean a lifetime of loneliness.